MARVEL

CAPTAIN AMERICA
THE WINTER SOLDIER
THE S.H.I.E.L.D. REPORT

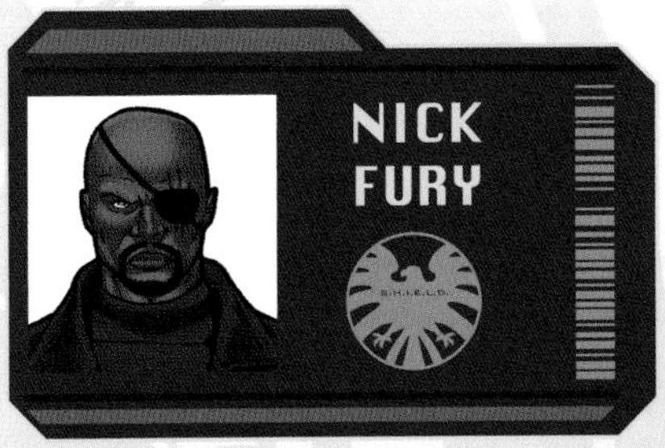
NICK
FURY
S.H.I.E.L.D.

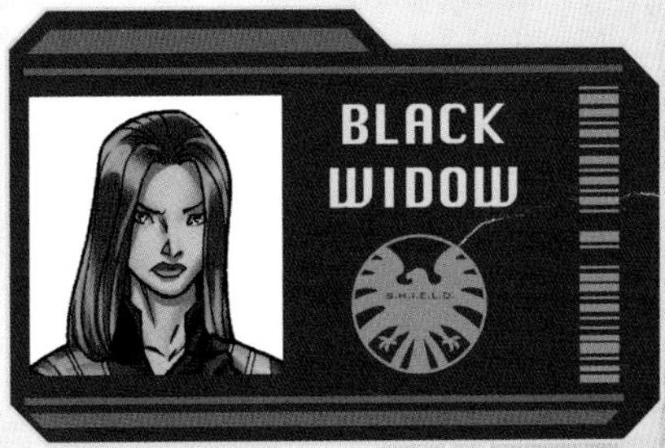
BLACK
WIDOW
S.H.I.E.L.D.

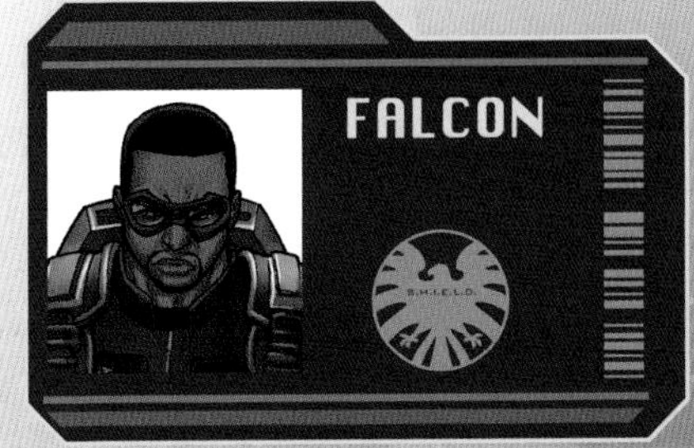
FALCON
S.H.I.E.L.D.

WRITTEN BY Tomas Palacios

BASED ON THE SCREENPLAY BY Christopher Markus & Stephen McFeely

PRODUCED BY Kevin Feige, p.g.a.

DIRECTED BY Anthony and Joe Russo

ILLUSTRATED BY Ron Lim, Cam Smith, & Lee Duhig

MARVEL
NEW YORK · LOS ANGELES

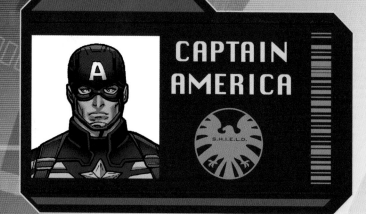

CAPTAIN AMERICA

S.H.I.E.L.D.

MARIA HILL

S.H.I.E.L.D.

ALEXANDER PIERCE

S.H.I.E.L.D.

BROCK RUMLOW

S.H.I.E.L.D.

WINTER SOLDIER

MARVEL
marvelkids.com

© 2014 MARVEL

All rights reserved. Published by Marvel Press, an imprint of Disney Book Group. No part of this book may be reproduced or transmitted in any form or by any means, electronic or mechanical, including photocopying, recording, or by any information storage and retrieval system, without written permission from the publisher. For information address Marvel Press, 1101 Flower Street, Glendale, California 91201.

Printed in the United States of America

First Edition

1 3 5 7 9 10 8 6 4 2

F322-8368-0-14015

ISBN 978-1-4231-8535-2

S.H.I.E.L.D. COMMUNICATION

Agent: [redacted]

From: Agent Sitwell

Subject: Briefing Files

Agent [redacted],

During our recent investigation into the events that occurred in Washington, D.C., mainly the battle between Captain America and the one they call the Winter Soldier, we have compiled the following files for analysis. We need you to make sure all information has been reviewed thoroughly and that nothing has been missed. And I mean nothing. After careful consideration, we have agreed to allow **YOU** limited access.

The collection of this information has been accomplished through state-of-the-art nanocamera recorders, microscopic sound devices, CCTVs hacked by S.H.I.E.L.D. personnel, and much more. We have taken that info and compiled the following briefings that we will present to the World Security Council once you are done reviewing. This must **NOT** be discussed with anyone. This information is vital to the safety and longevity of the S.H.I.E.L.D. program . . . and the world.

Sincerely,

Agent Sitwell

STEVE ROGERS

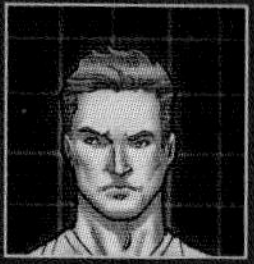

STEVE ROGERS was born on July 4, 1918, in Brooklyn, N.Y. He was a sickly child who struggled through his adolescent years with both his health and size. His one true friend, who helped him along the way and occasionally fought his schoolyard battles, was James Buchanan Barnes. (Please see **"The Winter Soldier"** file, page 46.) When the war came, Steve, a patriot through and through, wanted to join the fight against the Axis powers. But due to his poor physical condition, he was denied enlistment again and again. Bucky, on the other hand, was not and planned to serve overseas as a ground trooper.

Steve attended the World Exhibition of Tomorrow, where, with one last bit of hope in his heart, he entered a recruiting center. There he met Dr. Erskine, a scientist who told Steve he could get him into the army, but it would involve being part of a special project.

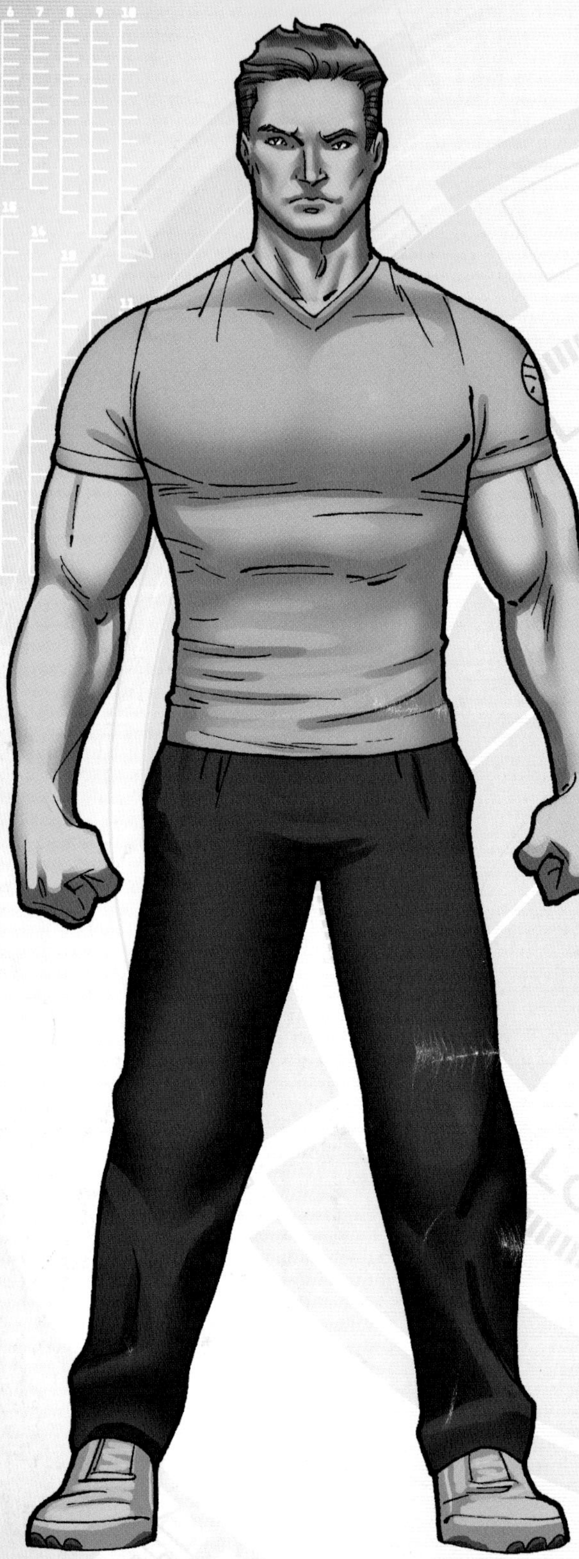

Steve accepted the offer, and after a series of tests, chemical realignment, and Vita-Ray exposure, he was transformed into the world's first Super-Soldier. (See **Captain America** file, page 6.)

STEVE IS FASTER, STRONGER, AND MORE AGILE THAN THE MOST FIT HUMAN.

S.H.I.E.L.D.

"Because the strong man who has known power all his life may lose respect for that power, but a weak man knows the value of strength and compassion."

CAPTAIN AMERICA: THE FIRST AVENGER

STEVE ROGERS became known as Captain America: the First Avenger. Cap (as he would be called on occasion) battled across Europe, taking down the lethal force known as HYDRA, which was led by its maniacal leader, Johann Schmidt, aka the Red Skull. After confronting the Red Skull and thwarting his plans to destroy America with deadly hydrogen bombs, Cap heroically sacrificed himself and crash-landed the bomb-carrying aircraft into the Antarctic, where he lay buried in the thick ice for over half a century, untouched, leaving behind the woman he loved, Peggy Carter. Following Steve's crash, Ms. Carter, a lieutenant with the SSR (Strategic Scientific Reserve—**ACCESS TO FILE DENIED**), eventually moved on with her life. She married, had children, and is now retired from active duty. (Files on Peggy Carter have been removed from report per Steve Rogers's orders.)

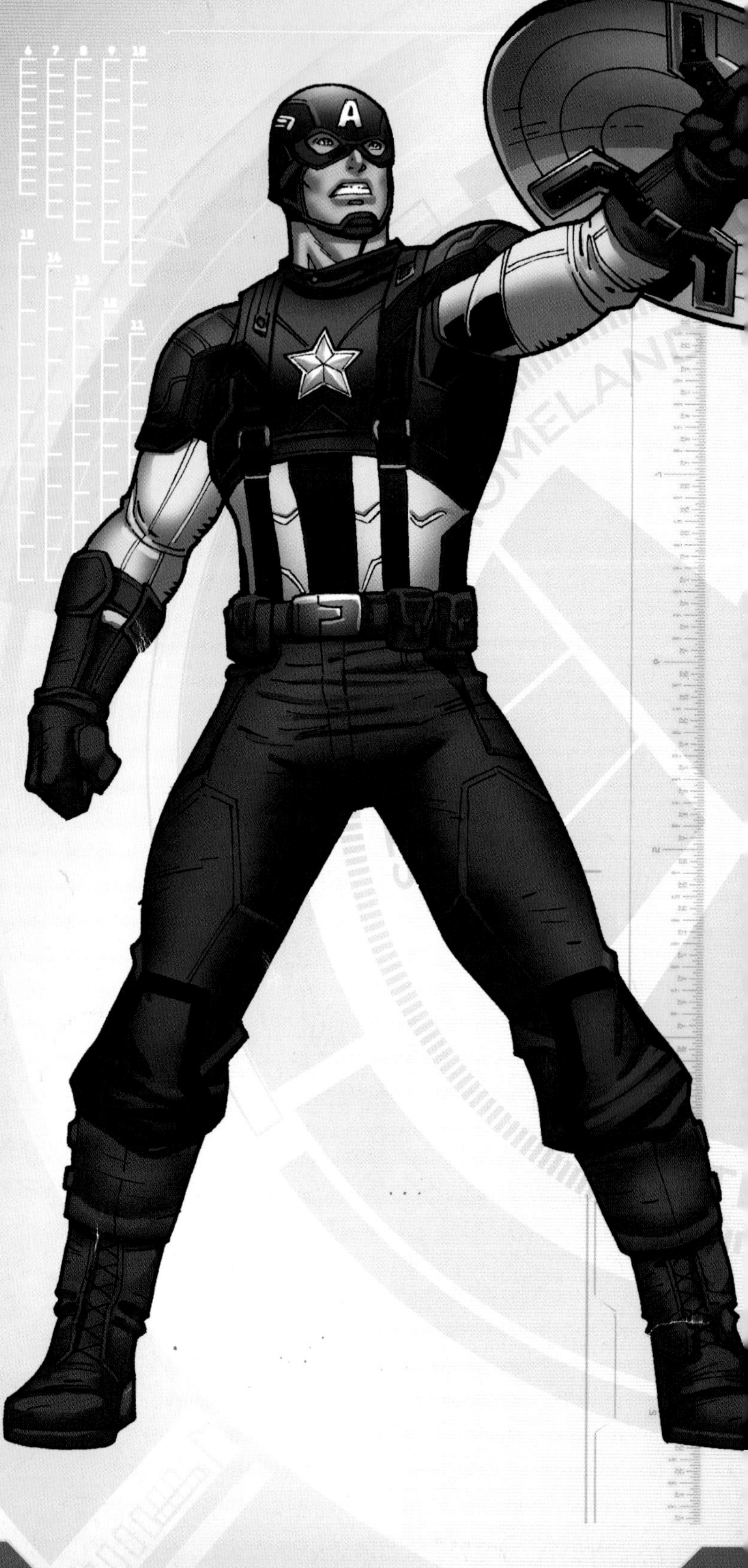

{798 DIDOT-PUNKTE=300MM}
DIDOT-PUNKT*0.3759398=MM
DIDOT-PUNKT*1.87001=PICA-PUNKT
DIDOT-PUNKT*0.0148057=INCH

Decades later, S.H.I.E.L.D. discovered Captain America within the depths of the ocean. For Steve Rogers, adapting to life in the twenty-first century after being frozen for seventy years was quite a challenge. But when he donned the Captain America suit again, his training came back to him naturally. He was ready to jump back into action for our country once again.

Captain America joined forces with several other Super Heroes: Iron Man, Thor, Hulk, and S.H.I.E.L.D. agents Black Widow (see **Natasha Romanoff/Black Widow** file, page 14) and Hawkeye. Together, under the direction of Nick Fury (see **Nick Fury** and **S.H.I.E.L.D.** file, page 18), they formed a formidable team: the Avengers.

Following the Avengers' victorious battle in New York City against Loki and the alien race the Chitauri, Steve Rogers began to settle into his new life in the modern world. After attempting to adapt to new advancements in technology and understand the world in general, Steve set forth to "catch up" to modern times. To help with this task, Steve began a new life as a S.H.I.E.L.D. agent, reporting directly to S.H.I.E.L.D. Director Nick Fury and learning about the ever-changing world through his counterparts.

FILE FOOTAGE OF STEVE ROGERS

PROPERTY OF
S.H.I.E.L.D.

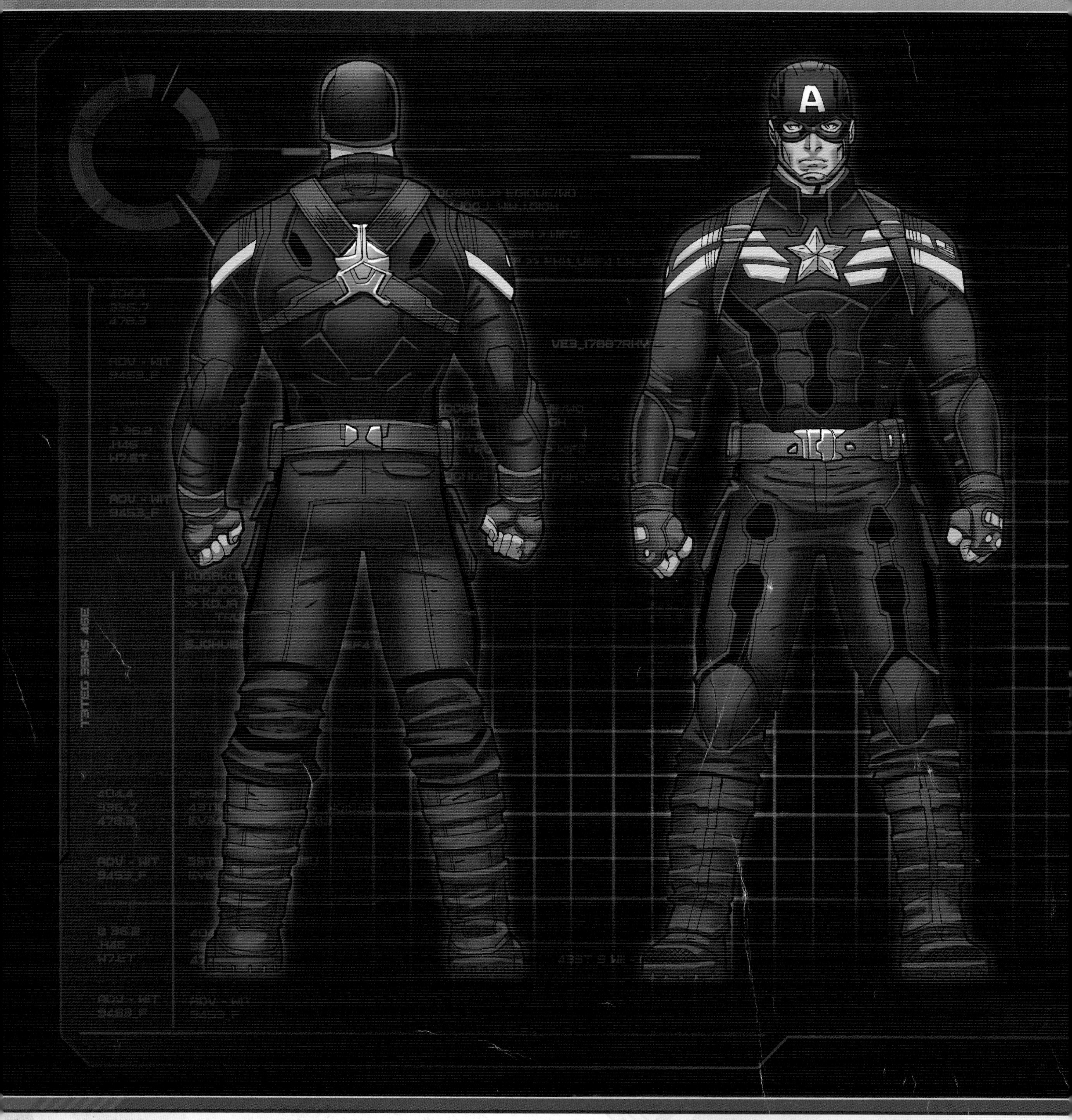

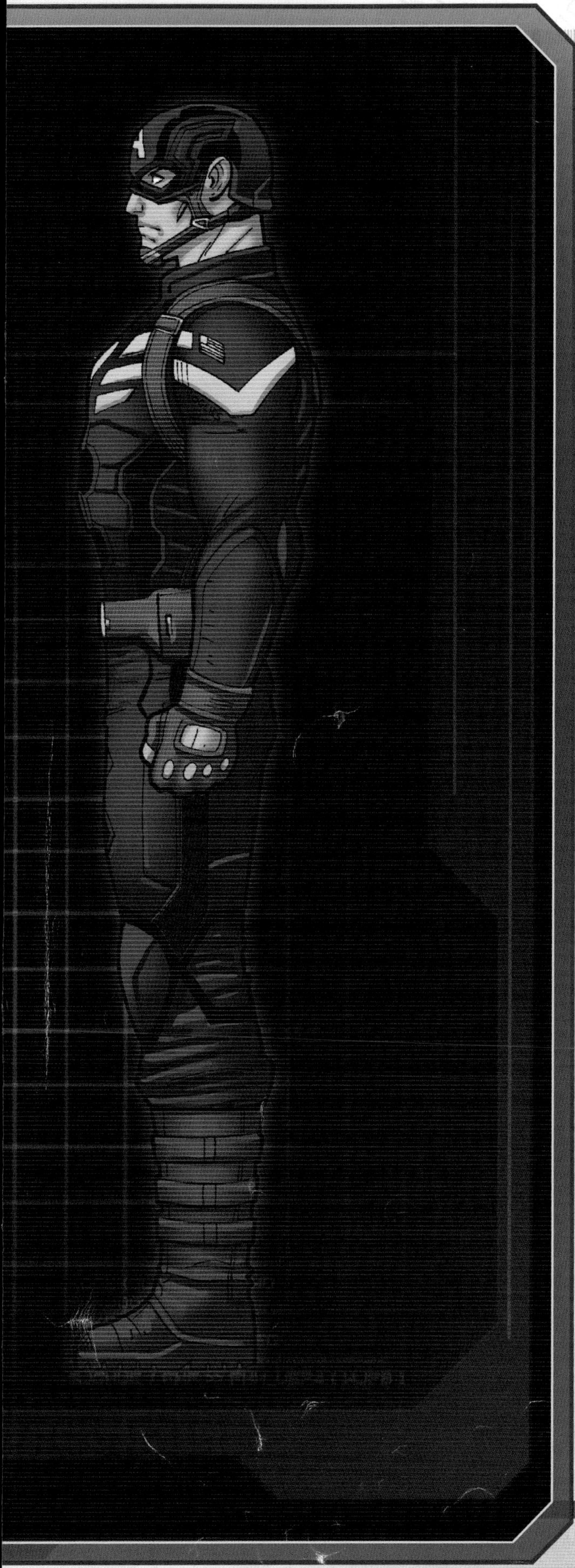

CAPTAIN AMERICA: STEALTH COSTUME

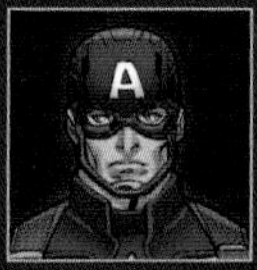

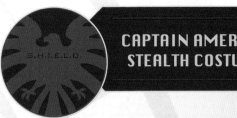

EQUIPPED WITH A STREAMLINED UNIFORM and his Vibranium shield, Captain America led a team of covert S.H.I.E.L.D. operatives on clandestine missions into the most threatening areas of the globe. Missions came directly from Nick Fury, and Cap's team usually consisted of Black Widow, Brock Rumlow, and Rumlow's elite S.T.R.I.K.E. unit.

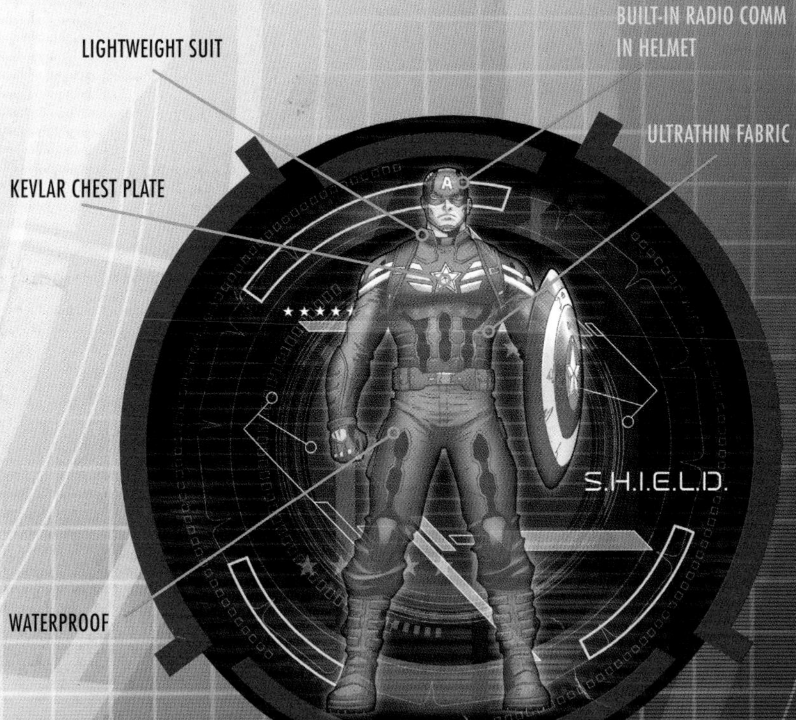

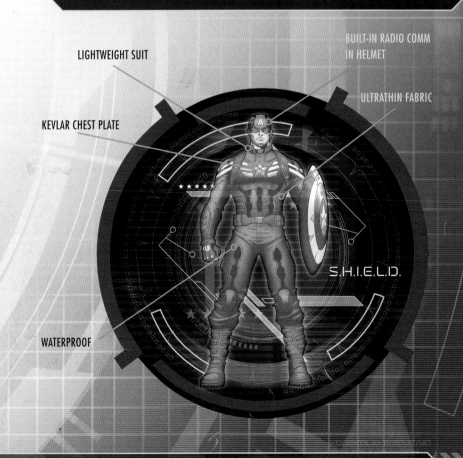

LIGHTWEIGHT SUIT
BUILT-IN RADIO COMM IN HELMET
ULTRATHIN FABRIC
KEVLAR CHEST PLATE
WATERPROOF
S.H.I.E.L.D.

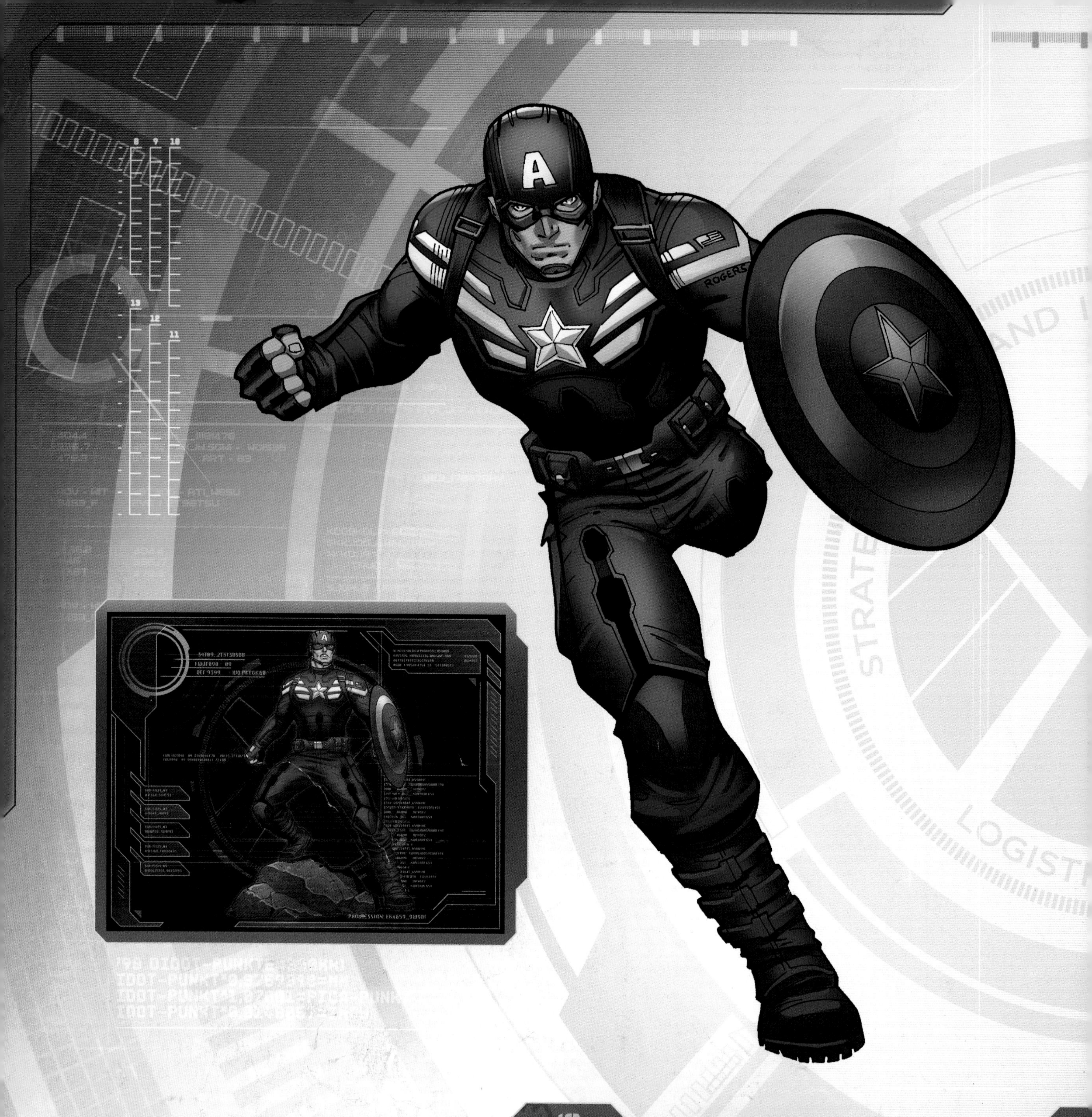
ROGERS

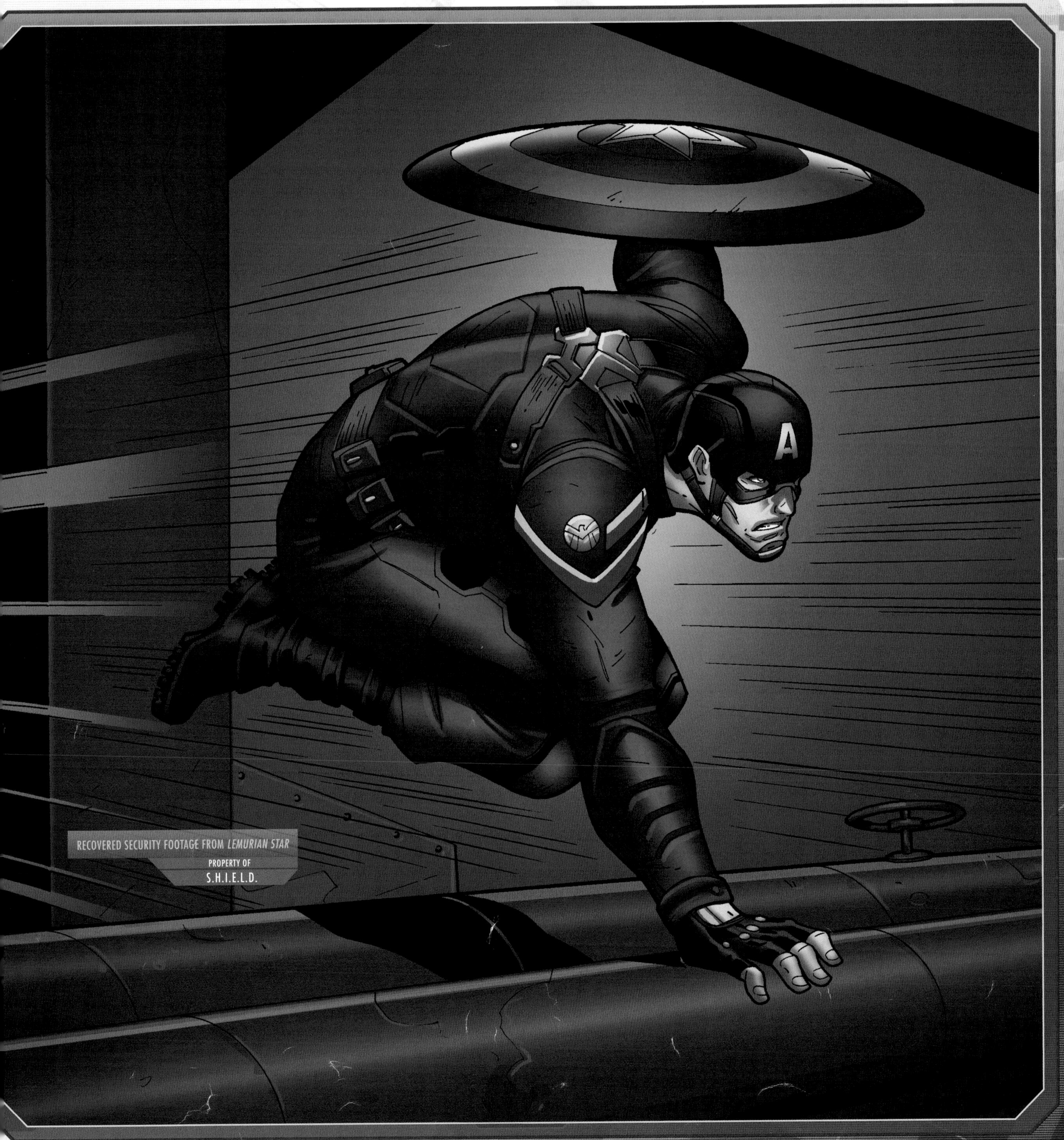
RECOVERED SECURITY FOOTAGE FROM *LEMURIAN STAR*
PROPERTY OF
S.H.I.E.L.D.

CAPTAIN AMERICA'S SHIELD

THE FIRST VERSION of Cap's shield was a stage prop when Captain America was in the USO. Made of cheap metal, it served little purpose in the war. But that changed when Tony Stark's father, Howard, was tasked with creating both a weapon and a symbol for Captain America. Secretly working for the Strategic Scientific Reserve (SSR), Howard Stark crafted Captain America's now-iconic red, white, and blue shield. The material it's made of, Vibranium, is a virtually indestructible element that absorbs vibrations of any kind. It's so sturdy it even withstood a blow from Thor's hammer, Mjolnir. Recently, the shield received a makeover. Refinished with a sleeker color scheme, the stealth shield is perfect when needed for top-secret covert missions. Recently, the shield accompanied Cap on his hostage mission on the *Lemurian Star*.

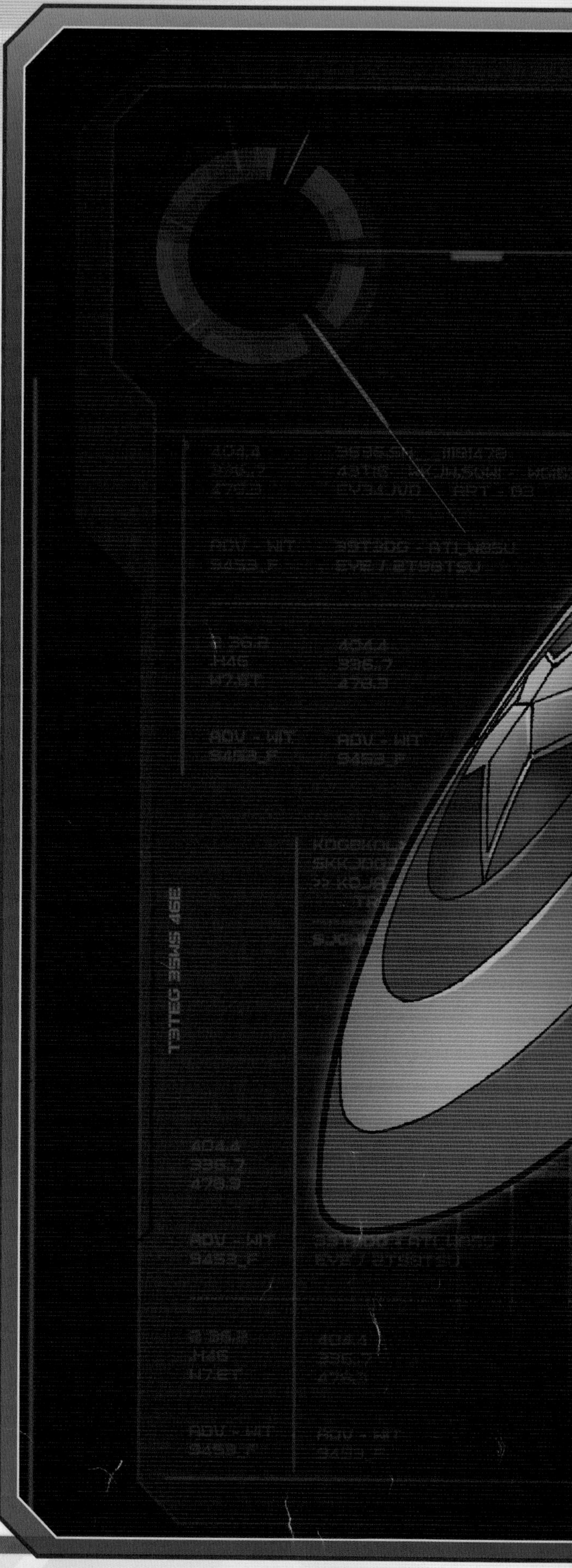

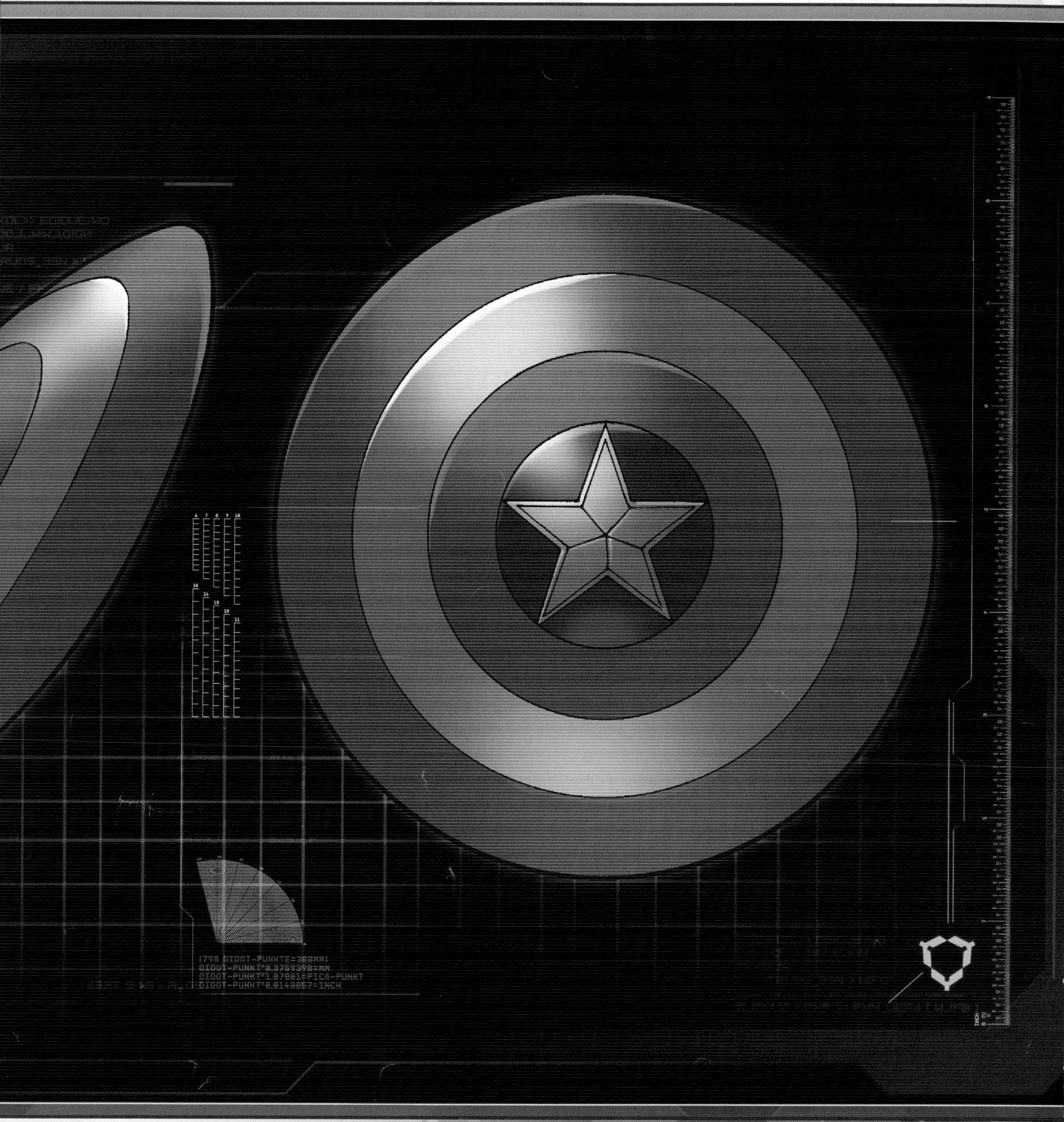
[798 DIDOT-PUNKTE=300MM]
DIDOT-PUNKT*0.3759398=MM
DIDOT-PUNKT*1.07001=PICA-PUNKT
DIDOT-PUNKT*0.0148057=INCH

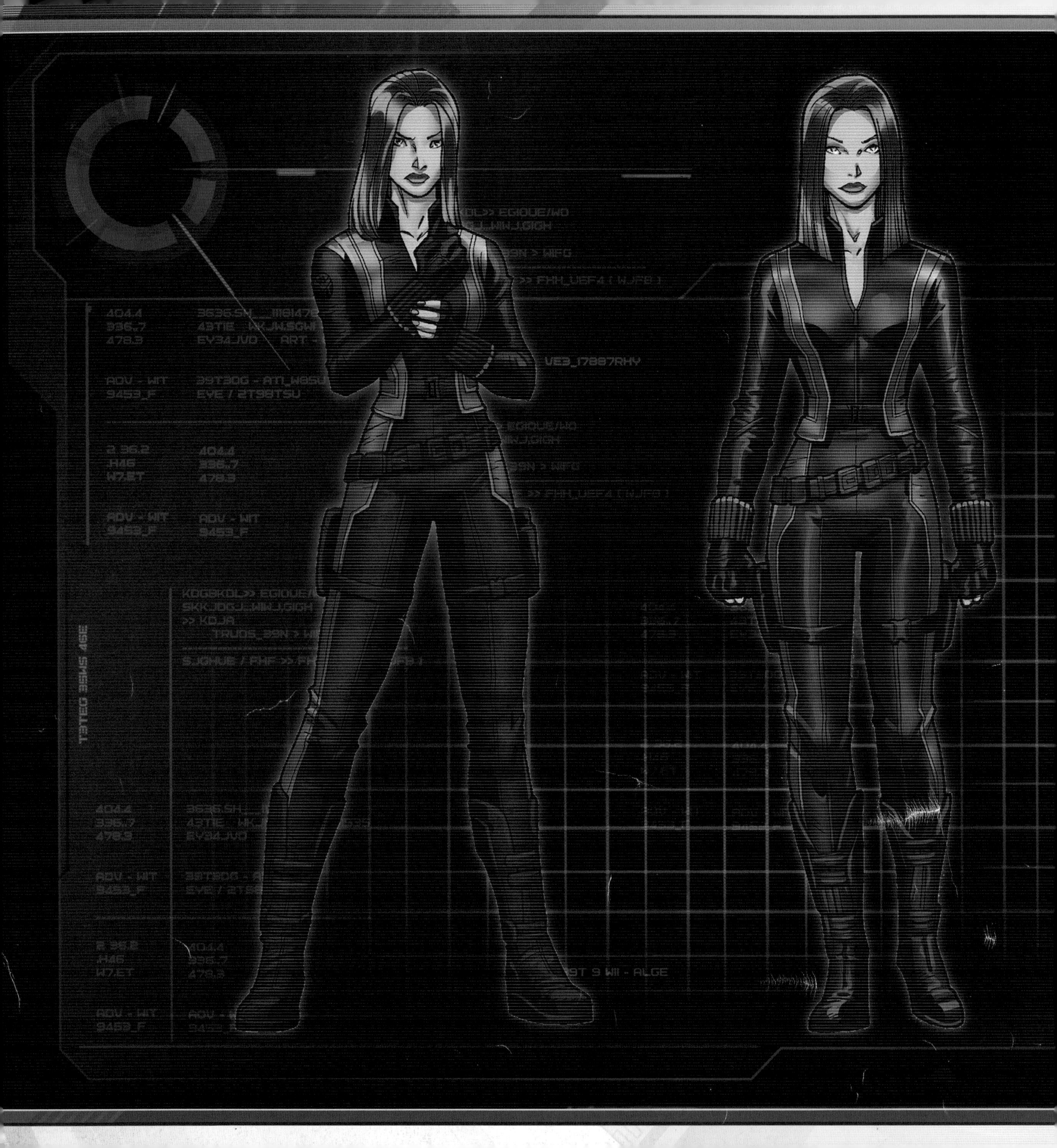

NATASHA ROMANOFF / BLACK WIDOW

AFTER FIGHTING ALONGSIDE her fellow Avengers in the Battle of New York, S.H.I.E.L.D. agent and super spy Natasha Romanoff returned to the sort of covert espionage operations that originally earned her the imposing code name Black Widow. Natasha now runs Nick Fury's most confidential missions (see **Rumlow and S.T.R.I.K.E.** file, page 30), lending her precise, skillful martial arts, hand-to-hand combat expertise, and potent "Widow's Bites" (high-tech Tasers that dispense from her wristlets) to S.H.I.E.L.D.'s specialized S.T.R.I.K.E. team. Black Widow's latest mission involved rescuing hostages from the *Lemurian Star*, a ship that was located in the Indian Ocean.

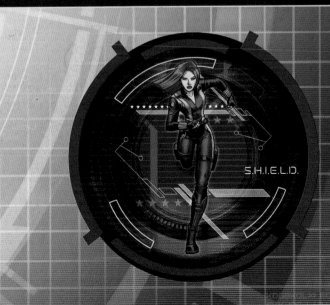

S.H.I.E.L.D.

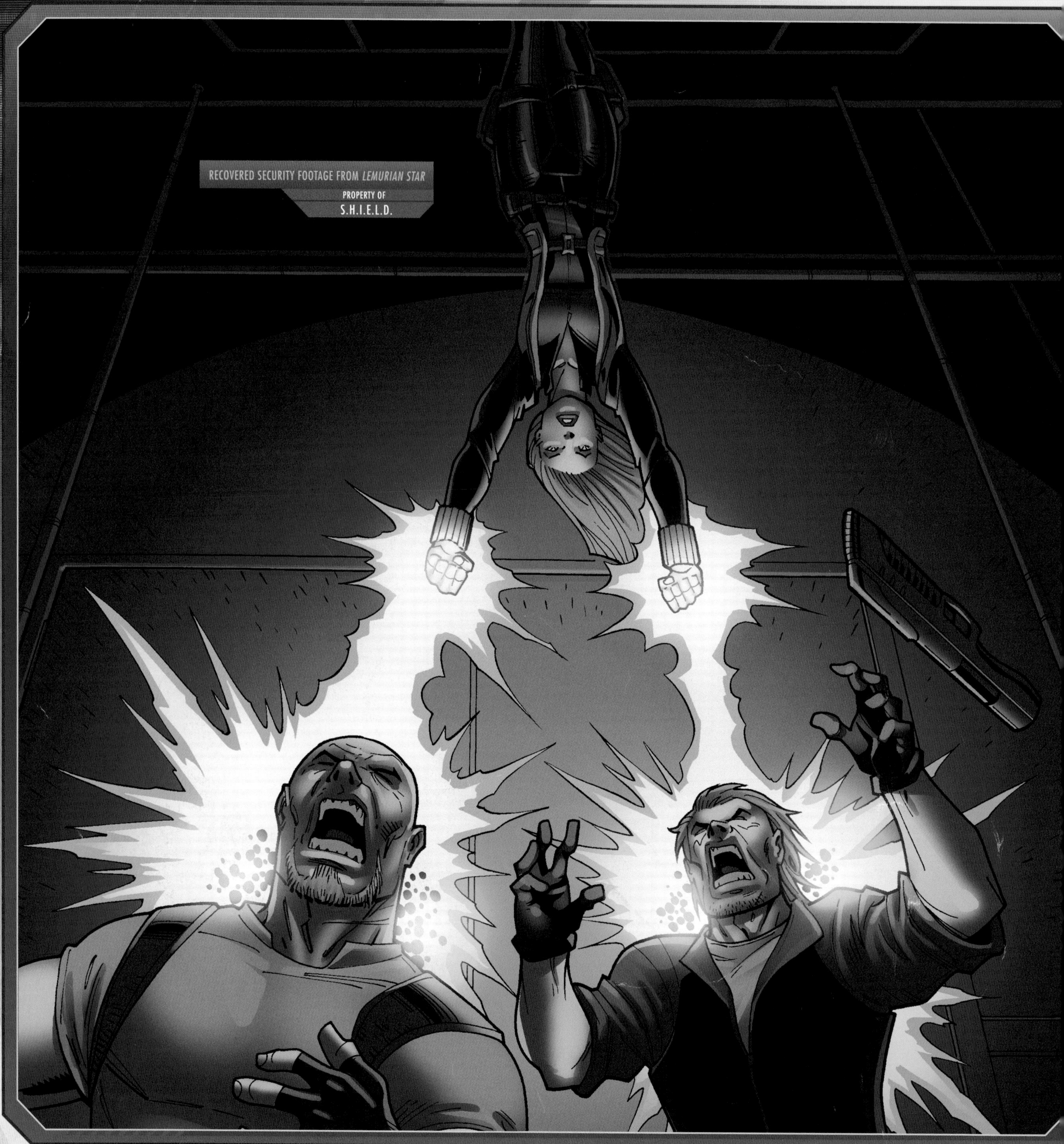
RECOVERED SECURITY FOOTAGE FROM *LEMURIAN STAR*
PROPERTY OF
S.H.I.E.L.D.

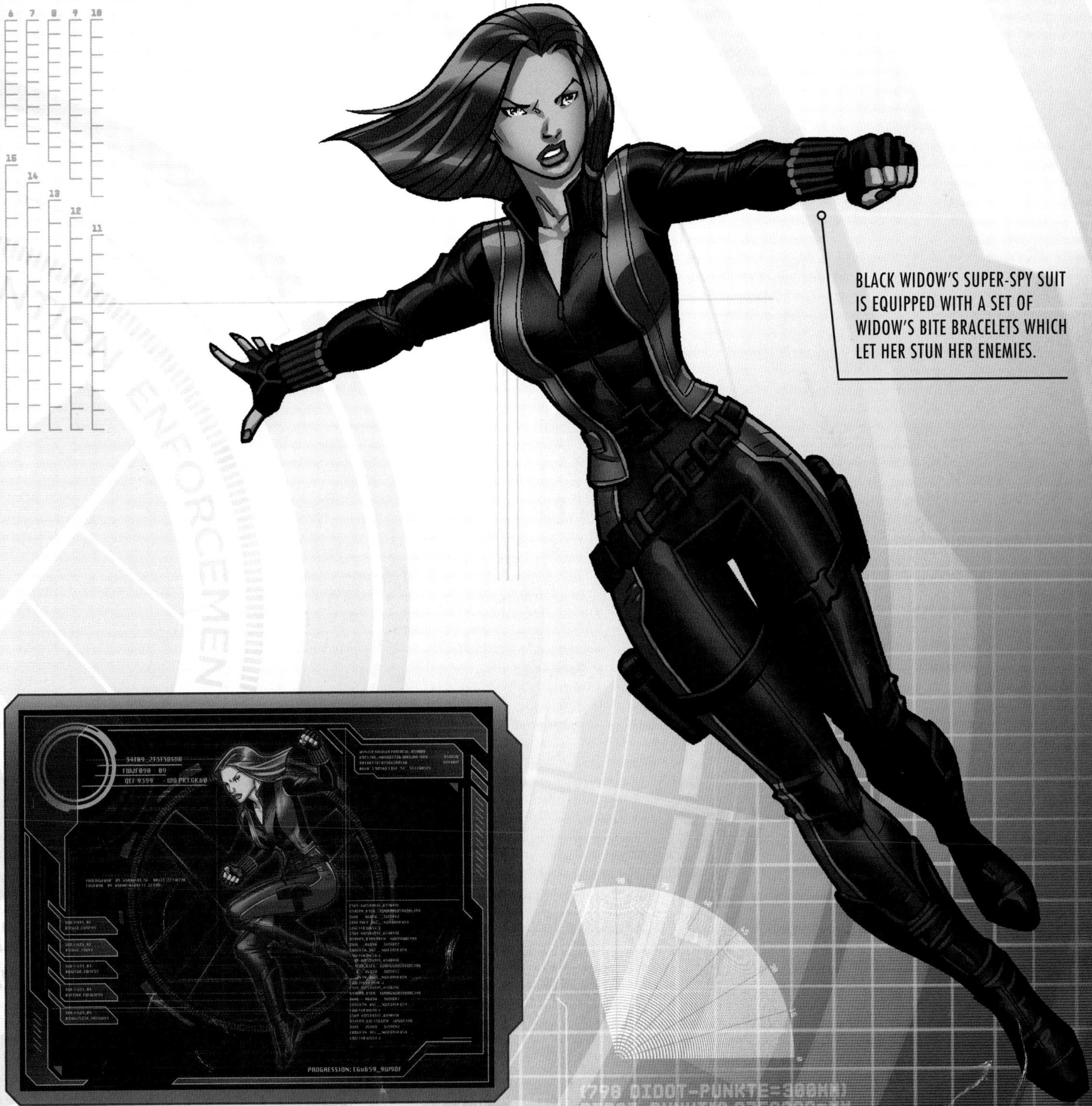

BLACK WIDOW'S SUPER-SPY SUIT IS EQUIPPED WITH A SET OF WIDOW'S BITE BRACELETS WHICH LET HER STUN HER ENEMIES.

NICK FURY AND S.H.I.E.L.D.

OVERSEEN BY THE WORLD SECURITY COUNCIL, the Strategic Homeland Intervention, Enforcement, and Logistics Division—or S.H.I.E.L.D.—is a global peacekeeping and intelligence organization that was created to stop threats against America and the world.

As Director of S.H.I.E.L.D., Nick Fury has his hands in everything from intelligence to defense. But his pet project is the "Avengers Initiative," an elite collective of super humans assembled to subdue global-scale threats that no single hero could face alone. Working from S.H.I.E.L.D.'s enormous flying headquarters, the Helicarrier (see **Helicarrier** file, page 36), Fury can quickly deploy the Avengers to handle any threat that may arise.

Fury has since commanded a small group of S.H.I.E.L.D. agents (Cap, Black Widow, and Rumlow) who handle covert and dangerous missions.

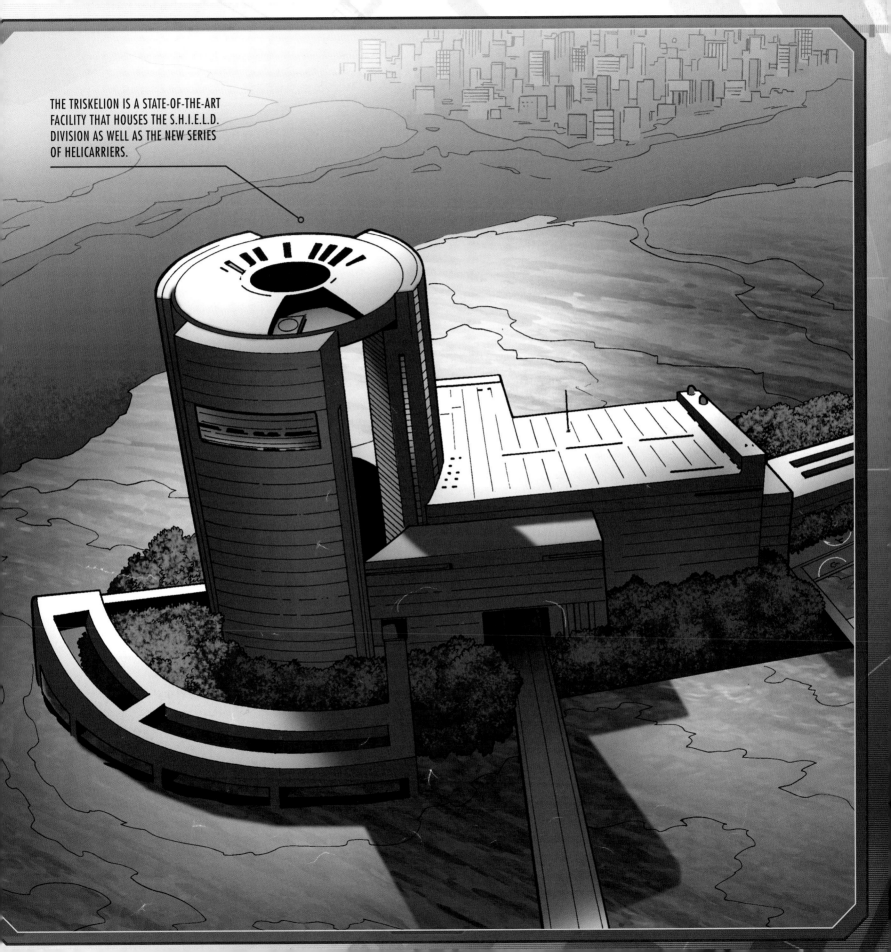

THE TRISKELION IS A STATE-OF-THE-ART FACILITY THAT HOUSES THE S.H.I.E.L.D. DIVISION AS WELL AS THE NEW SERIES OF HELICARRIERS.

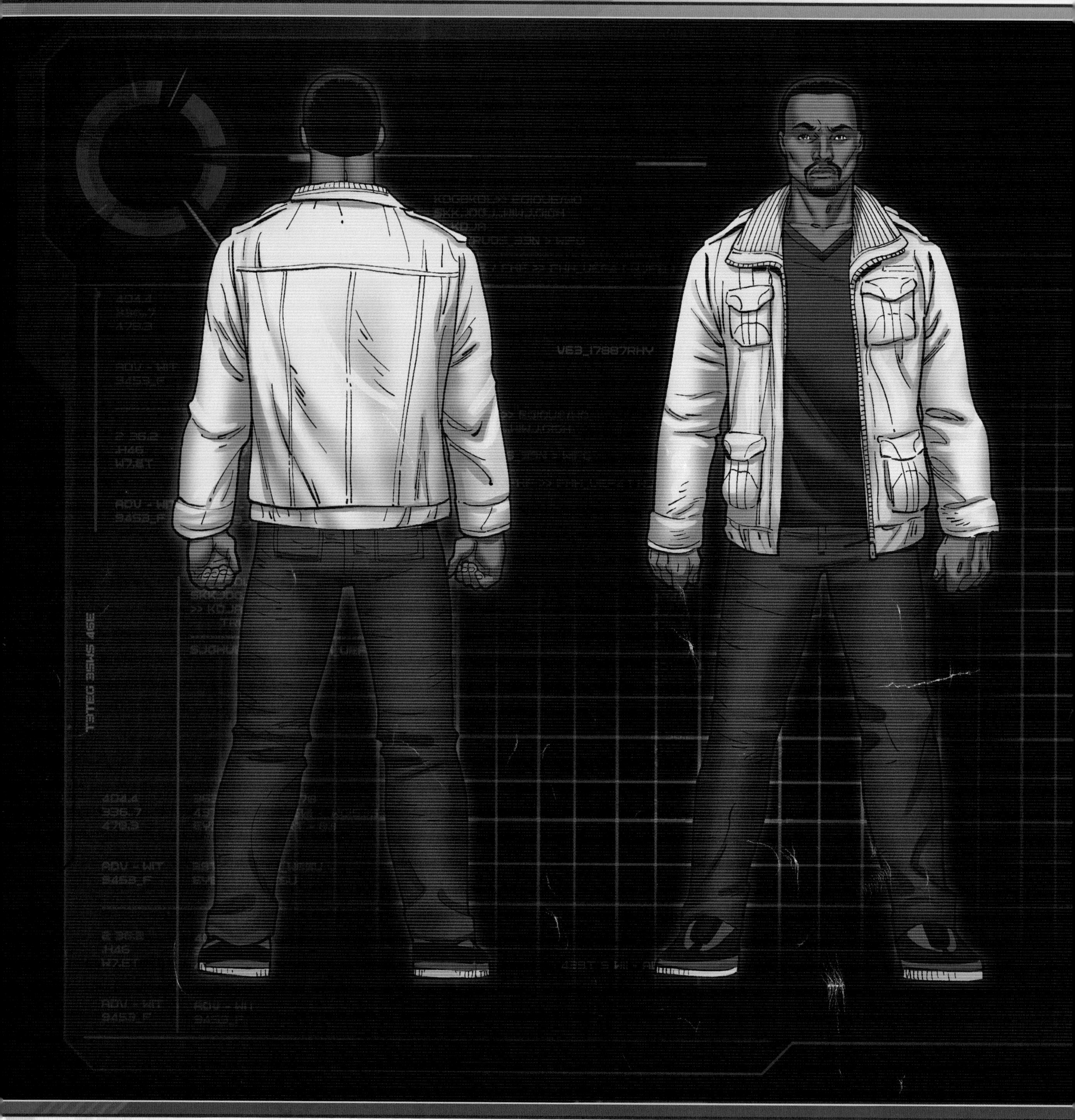

SAM WILSON

SAM WILSON first met Steve Rogers while jogging around the National Mall in Washington, D.C. The Super-Soldier literally ran laps around Sam before walking over and introducing himself. Sam recognized Steve and they shared the camaraderie of being soldiers and what that entails, such as the loss of a friend on the battlefield.

Sam served in the National Guard's 58th Pararescue Division along with his pararescue wingman, Riley. Five years ago, they were flying a night mission in Bakmala. It was a standard parajump rescue operation, something the duo had done more than a hundred times. But rebel forces spotted them and Riley was taken down by a rocket-propelled grenade launcher. Sam took the loss of Riley rather hard, but he learned to cope by volunteering as a counselor at the Department of Veterans Affairs in Washington, D.C. In that capacity, Sam proved to be a valuable ally in Steve Rogers's effort to acclimate to the modern era.

CODE NAME: FALCON

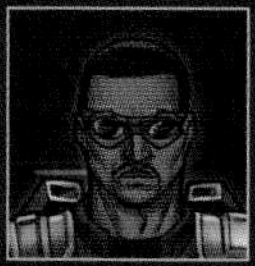

SAM DIDN'T HESITATE to suit up in the EXO-7 Falcon gear when Cap and Black Widow were in dire need of aid. The EXO-7 Falcon suit is an experimental flight harness equipped with polymer wings and numerous tactical armaments. It first took flight as part of Sam's Pararescue Division several years ago. Skilled in the use and limits (or lack thereof) of the suit, and with his considerable background in civilian rescue and combat abilities, Sam Wilson dons the suit and is now known as Falcon.

SUBJECT SAM WILSON REVEALS FALCON SUIT

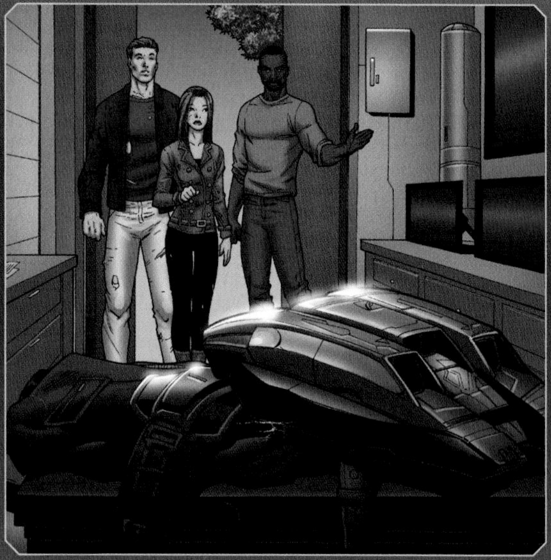

PROPERTY OF
S.H.I.E.L.D.

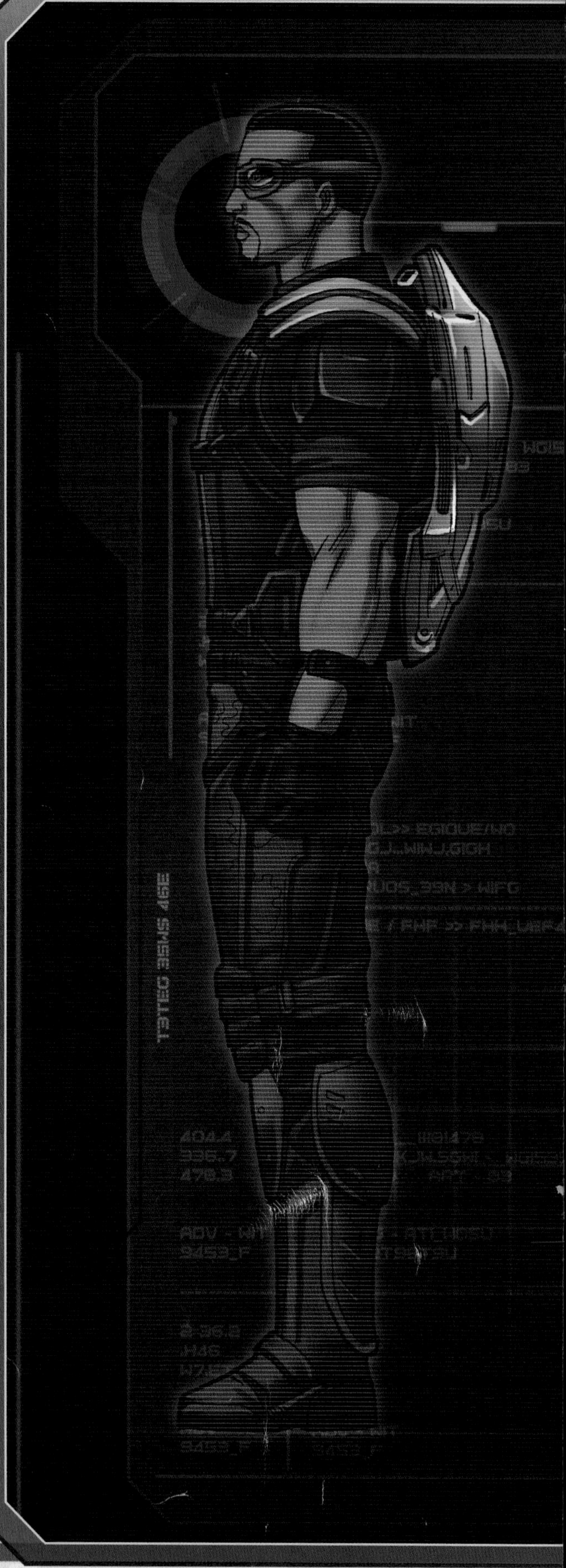

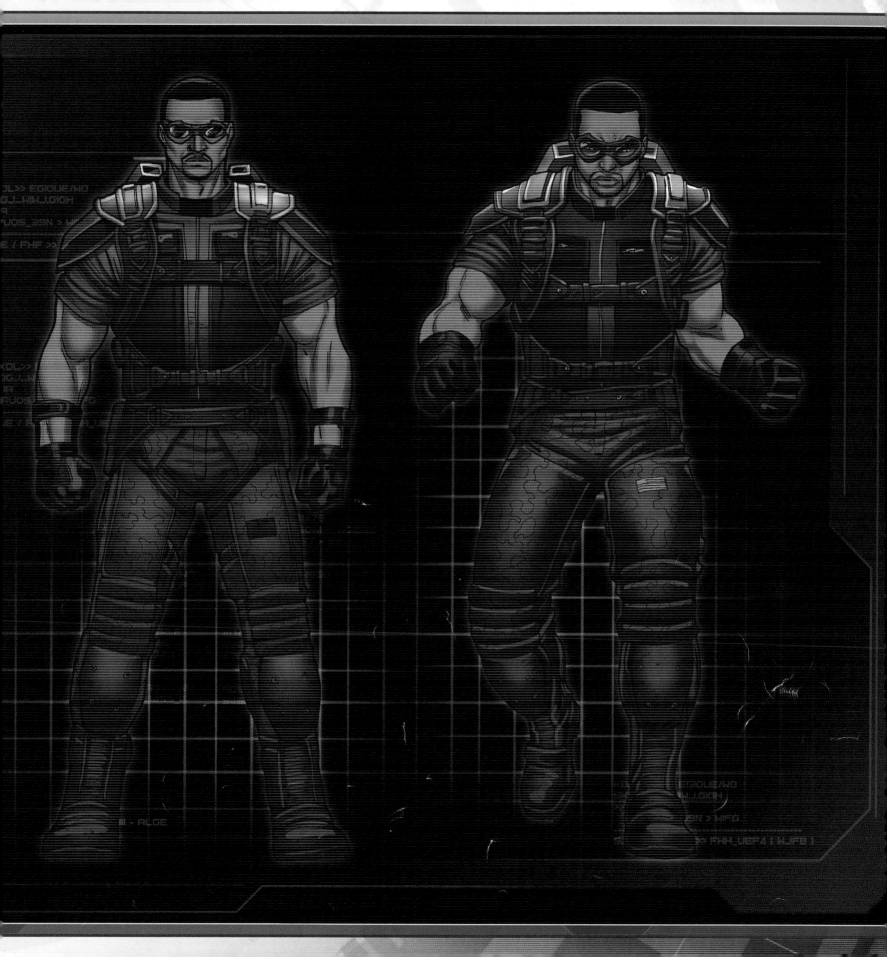

FALCON WINGS

THE EXO-7 FALCON SUIT is top-of-the-line technology. The wing harness features detachable glider wings made of lightweight material. The wings, with a span of over ten feet, can detach and reattach to the main uniform, which is made of synthetic stretch fabric lined with a steel-alloy mesh to help the wings maintain form when in flight.

SURVEILLANCE PHOTO OF FALCON IN ACTION AGAINST THE WINTER SOLDIER'S MERCENARIES.

PROPERTY OF
S.H.I.E.L.D.

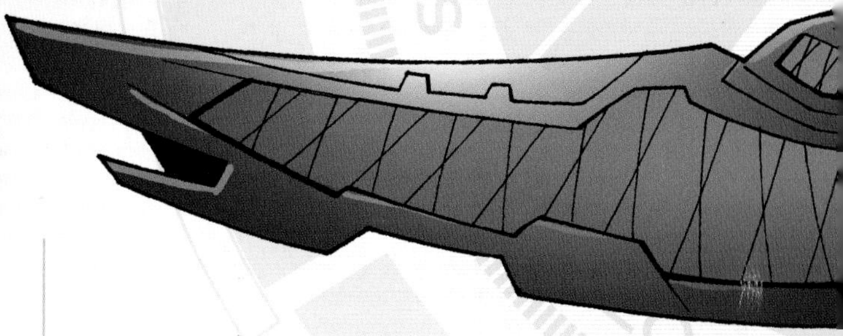

(798 DIDOT-PUNKTE=300MM)
DIDOT-PUNKT*0,3759398=MM
DIDOT-PUNKT*1,07001=PICA-PUNKT
DIDOT-PUNKT*0,0140057=INCH

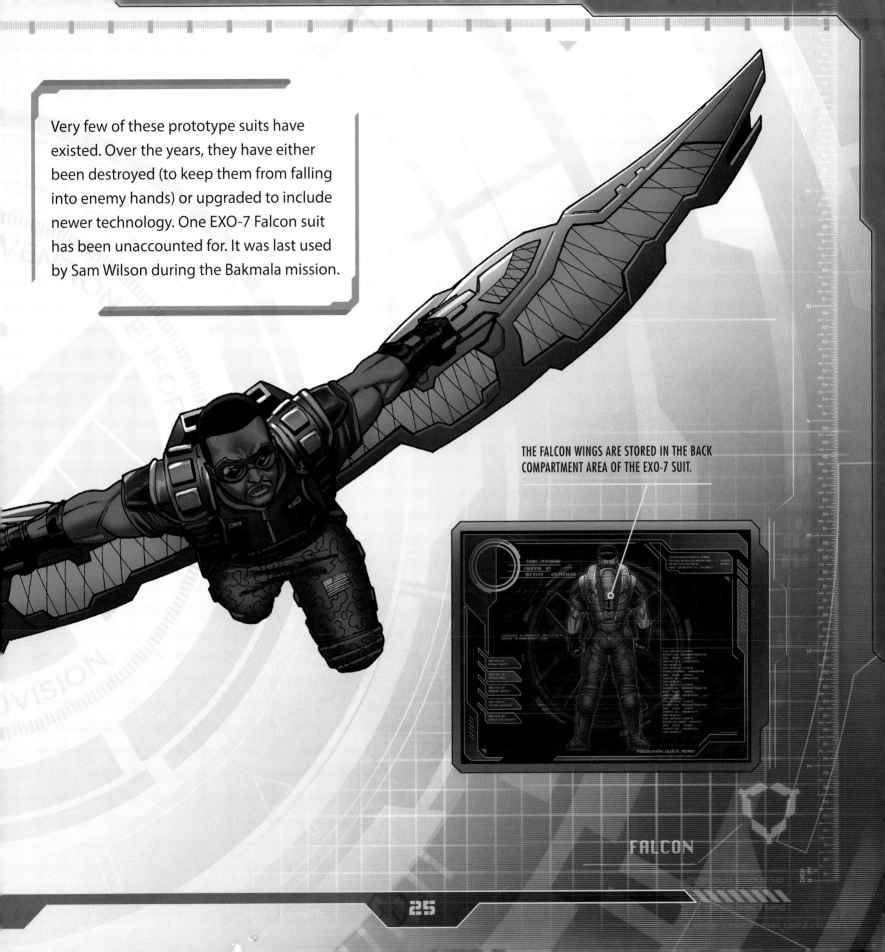

Very few of these prototype suits have existed. Over the years, they have either been destroyed (to keep them from falling into enemy hands) or upgraded to include newer technology. One EXO-7 Falcon suit has been unaccounted for. It was last used by Sam Wilson during the Bakmala mission.

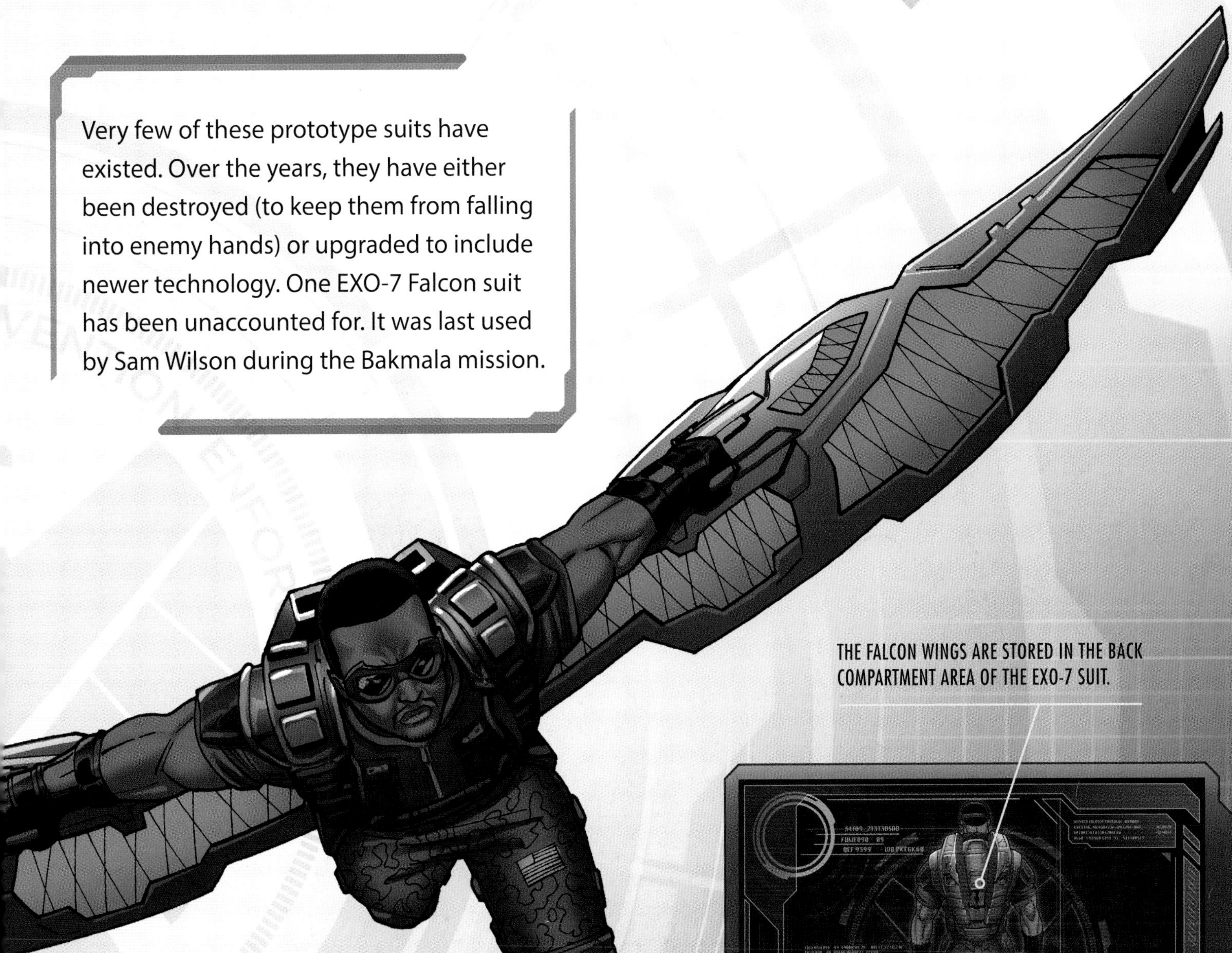

THE FALCON WINGS ARE STORED IN THE BACK COMPARTMENT AREA OF THE EXO-7 SUIT.

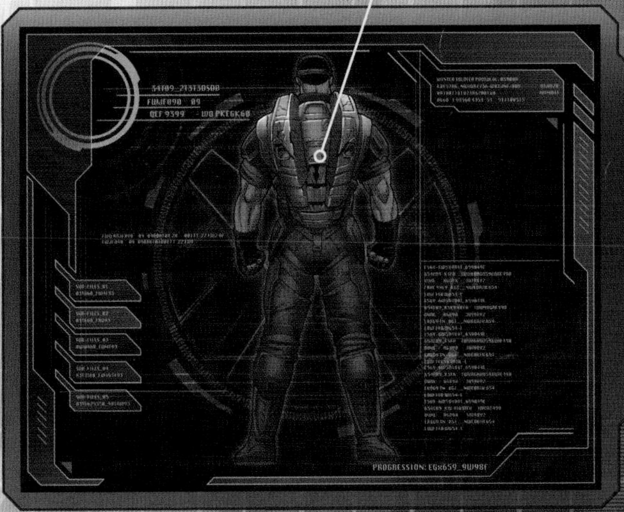

FALCON

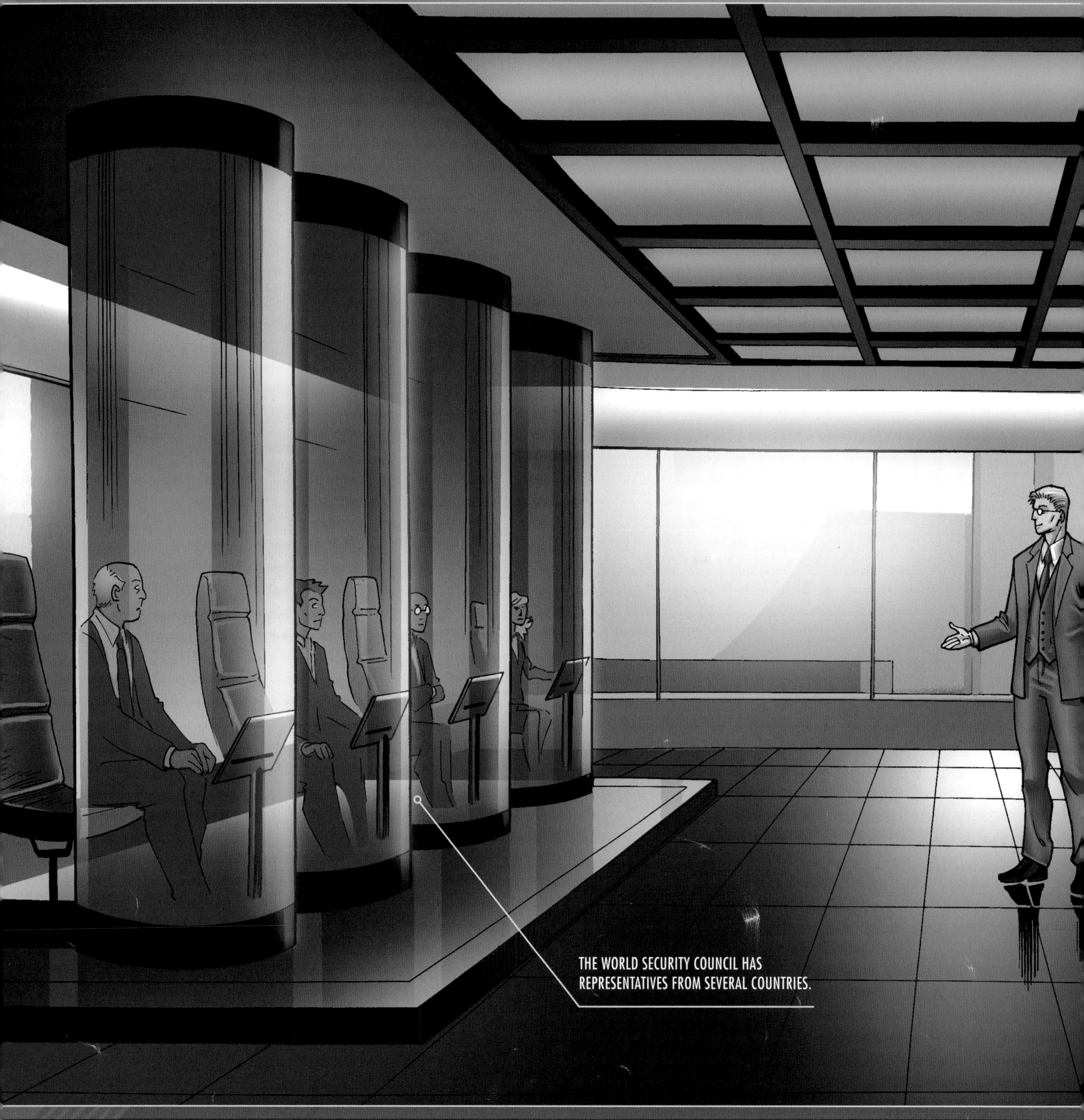
THE WORLD SECURITY COUNCIL HAS REPRESENTATIVES FROM SEVERAL COUNTRIES.

WORLD SECURITY COUNCIL

THE WORLD SECURITY COUNCIL consists of representatives from several major continents, including North America, Asia, and Europe. They are all powerful and all represent agendas for their respective countries. Most of the meetings happen fifty stories above the streets of Washington, D.C., in a high-tech room inside the Triskelion, where holograms project each country's delegate. Most meetings are led by Secretary Alexander Pierce, the liaison between the World Security Council and S.H.I.E.L.D. Topics range from the safety of the world to overseeing S.H.I.E.L.D. and how it operates.

Their latest meeting with Pierce involved the *Lemurian Star* and the hostage situation. The World Security Council was upset that a S.H.I.E.L.D. vessel had been hijacked by French pirates and they wanted to know why. More details will unfold throughout the week. Be on the lookout for reports regarding this matter.

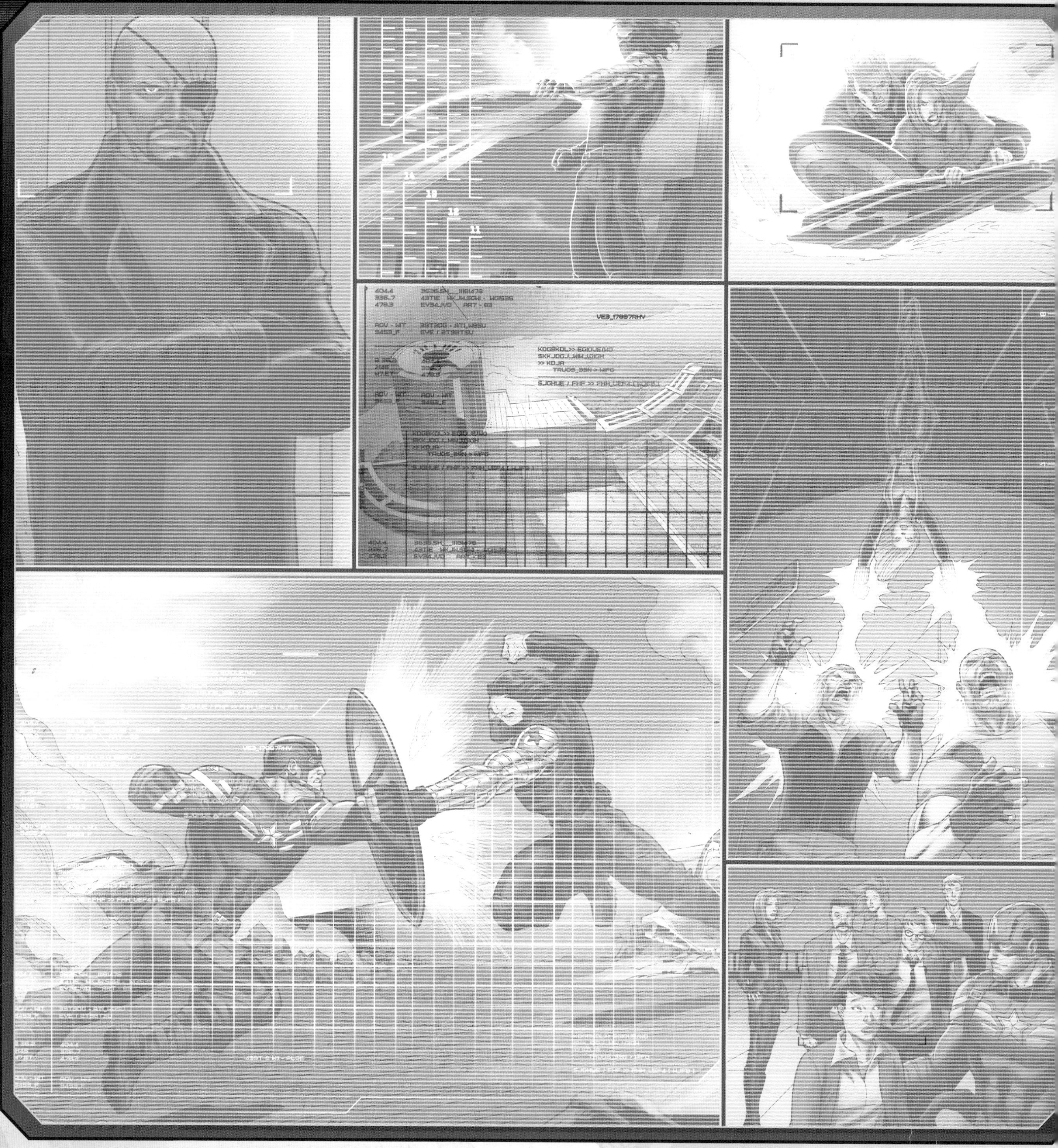
404.4 3636.SH__1181478
396.7 43TIE WK_I4LSGH : WG635
478.3 EV34JVD ART - 83
VE3_17987RHY
ADV - WT 397.DDG - ATI_W85U
9453_F EVE / 2T38TSU
KDGBKDL>> EGIOUE/HO
SKKJDDJ_NIW_IOIGH
>> KDJR
TRUOS_39N > WFG

ALEXANDER PIERCE

SECRETARY ALEXANDER PIERCE is the liaison between the World Security Council and S.H.I.E.L.D. He is also the man who swore in Nick Fury as the Director of S.H.I.E.L.D. Fury and Pierce share a history that is built on honor and respect. Pierce met Fury when he was working in the United States State Department of La Paz. An incident occurred where local rebels took the building and everyone inside hostage. With the help of his security detail, Pierce made it out, but his daughter did not. Fury approached Pierce with a plan to storm the building through the sewers. Pierce felt this was risky and wanted to negotiate with the rebels. Reports indicated that the rebel group, ELN, did not negotiate. The rebel leader gave the kill order and the rebels stormed down to the basement where the hostages had been held. When they got there, they found it empty. Nick Fury had ignored Pierce's direct orders and carried out an unauthorized military operation on foreign soil. In the process he saved every single hostage—including Pierce's daughter.

RUMLOW AND S.T.R.I.K.E.

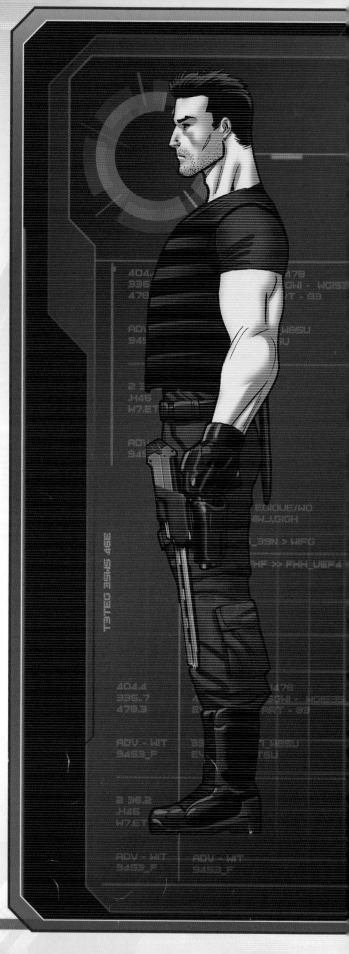

AGENT BROCK RUMLOW is part of the espionage team consisting of Captain America and Black Widow. Along with the S.T.R.I.K.E. team he commands, Rumlow answers the call to every mission given to him by Director Fury. With a vast arsenal of high-tech weaponry at his disposal, as well as the Quinjet, Rumlow is a force to be reckoned with. Like Black Widow, Rumlow specializes in various forms of martial arts and hand-to-hand combat and is an excellent marksman. Rumlow has seen the battlefield numerous times and works well under pressure. He recently assisted in saving the hostages from the *Lemurian Star*. Agent Rumlow's next mission is finding the Winter Soldier and his mercs.

S.T.R.I.K.E.

404.4
336.7
478.3
ADV - WIT
9453_F
ADV - WIT
9453_F

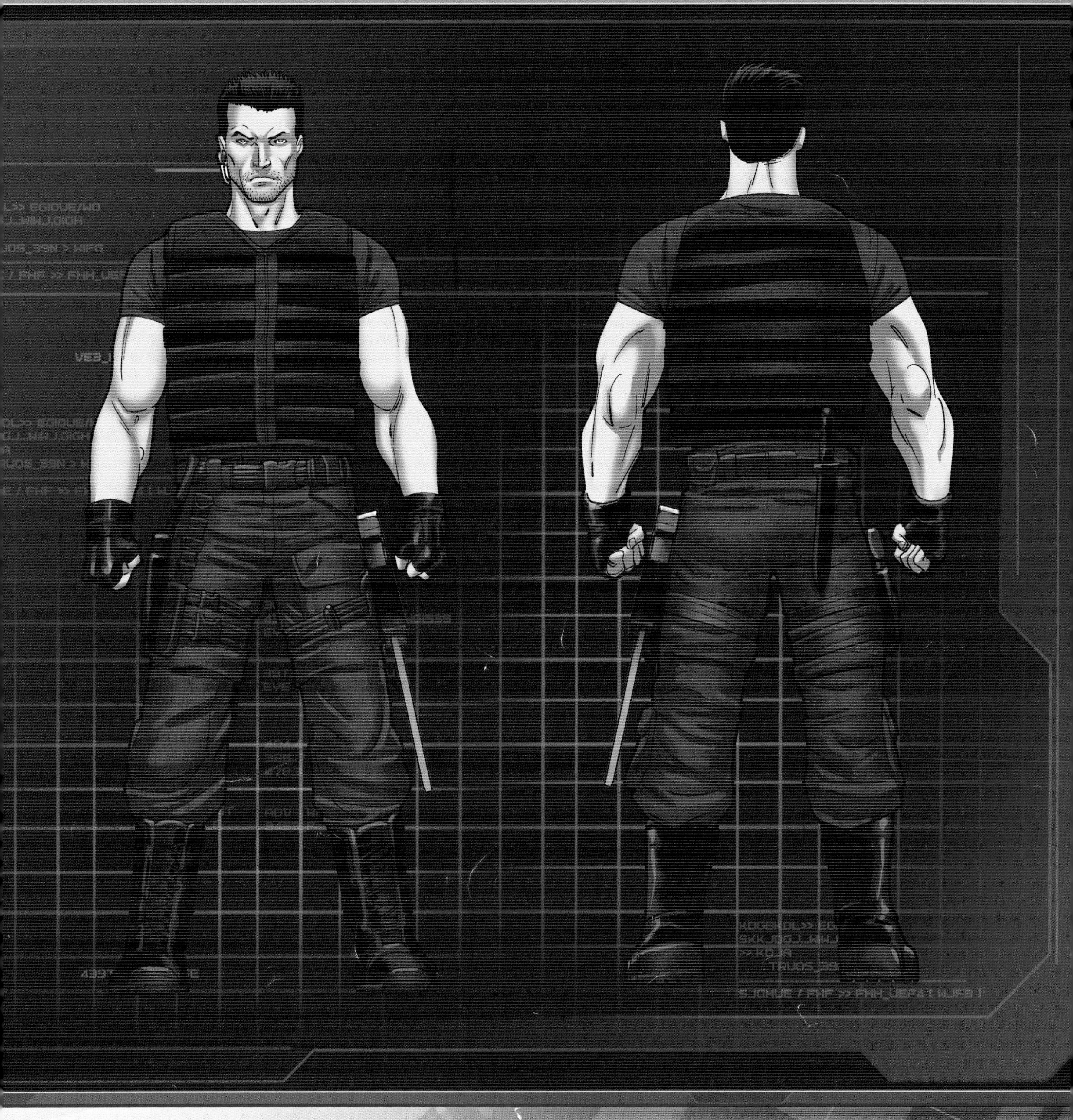

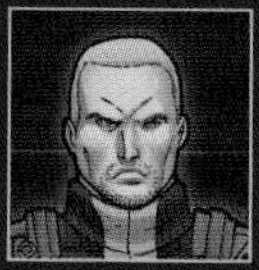

BATROC AND FOOT SOLDIERS

GEORGES BATROC: an ex-member of the French government agency in the action division. He has notched thirty-six high-profile missions from Serbia to Russia and led a team of some of the world's top mercenaries. He is highly dangerous and will stop at nothing to get what he wants, including taking S.H.I.E.L.D.'s Satellite Launch Platform Vessel, known as the *Lemurian Star*, and everyone on it hostage. He demanded a ransom of $1.5 billion. However, S.H.I.E.L.D. does not negotiate. Instead we sent in Captain America, Black Widow, and Agent Rumlow to take back the vessel. The covert operation was a success, with Batroc meeting the blunt force of Cap's boot and shield. Granted, we rescued the hostages and regained the ship, but Rumlow escaped, not before causing an intense explosion that ripped through the control room.

Batroc was picked up in a safe house in Algiers. He is now being held in a S.H.I.E.L.D. interrogation compound, where he will be questioned as to who put him up to the *Lemurian* hostage situation, as well as the recent incident involving Nick Fury.

BATROC'S TEAM CONSISTS OF HIGHLY TRAINED SOLDIERS SKILLED IN COMBAT AND WEAPONRY.

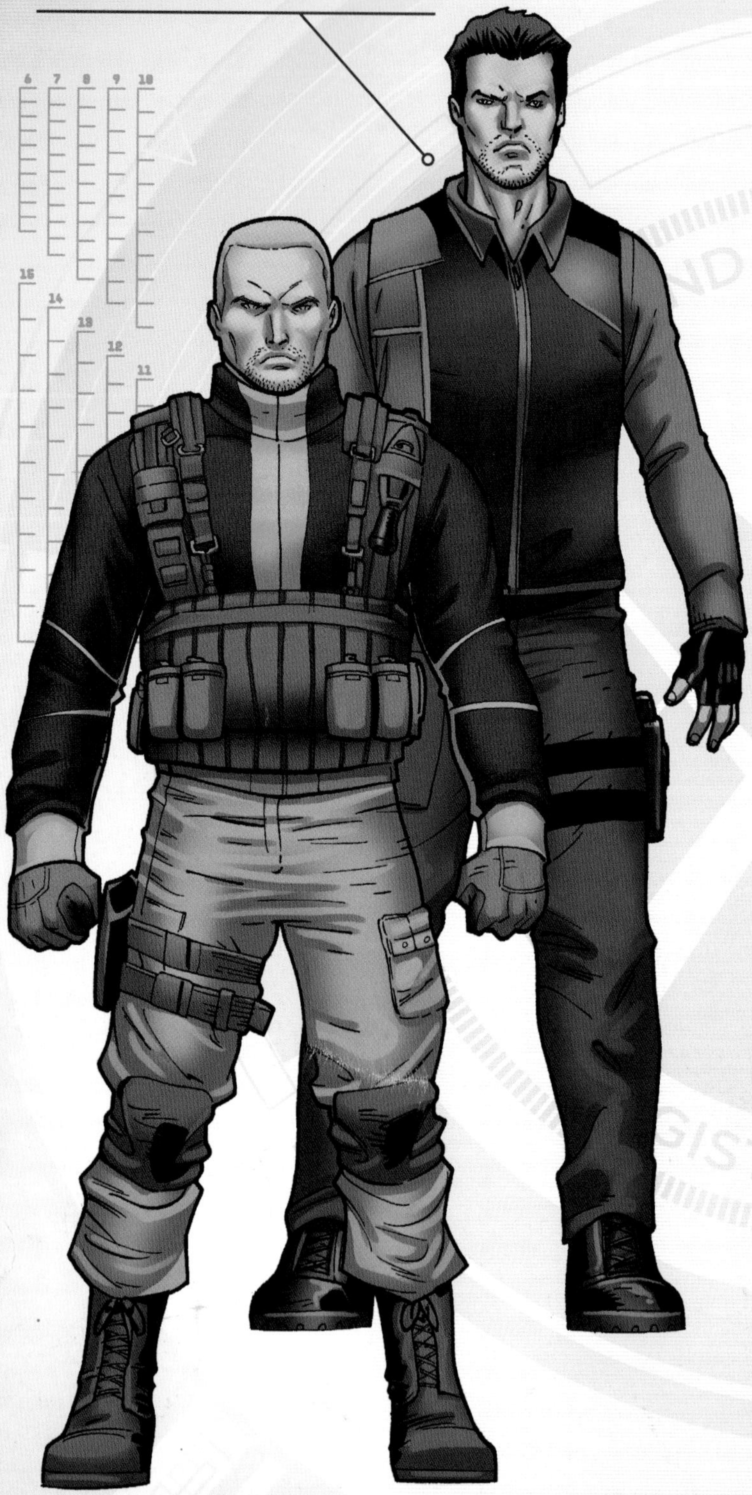

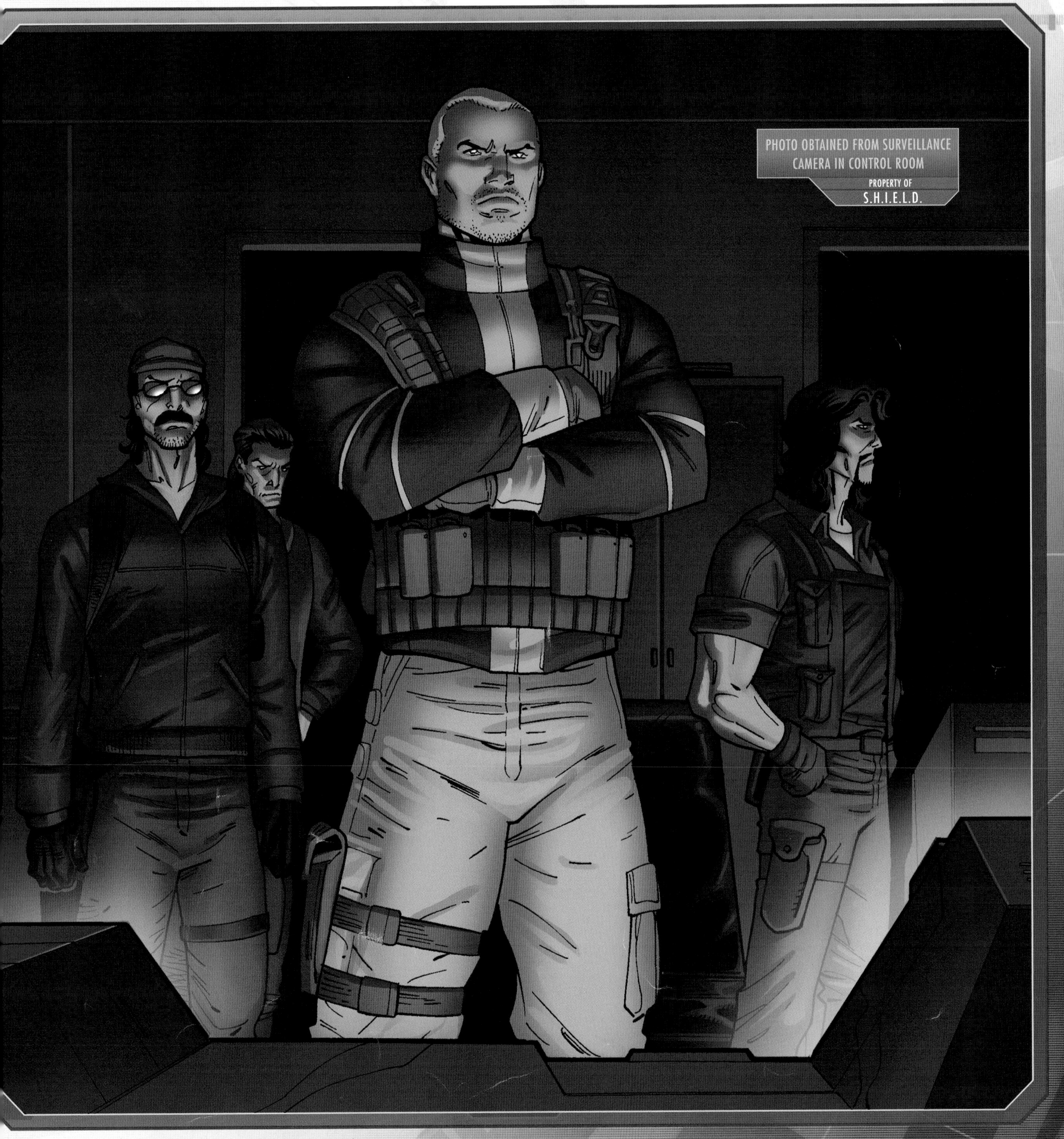
PHOTO OBTAINED FROM SURVEILLANCE CAMERA IN CONTROL ROOM
PROPERTY OF
S.H.I.E.L.D.

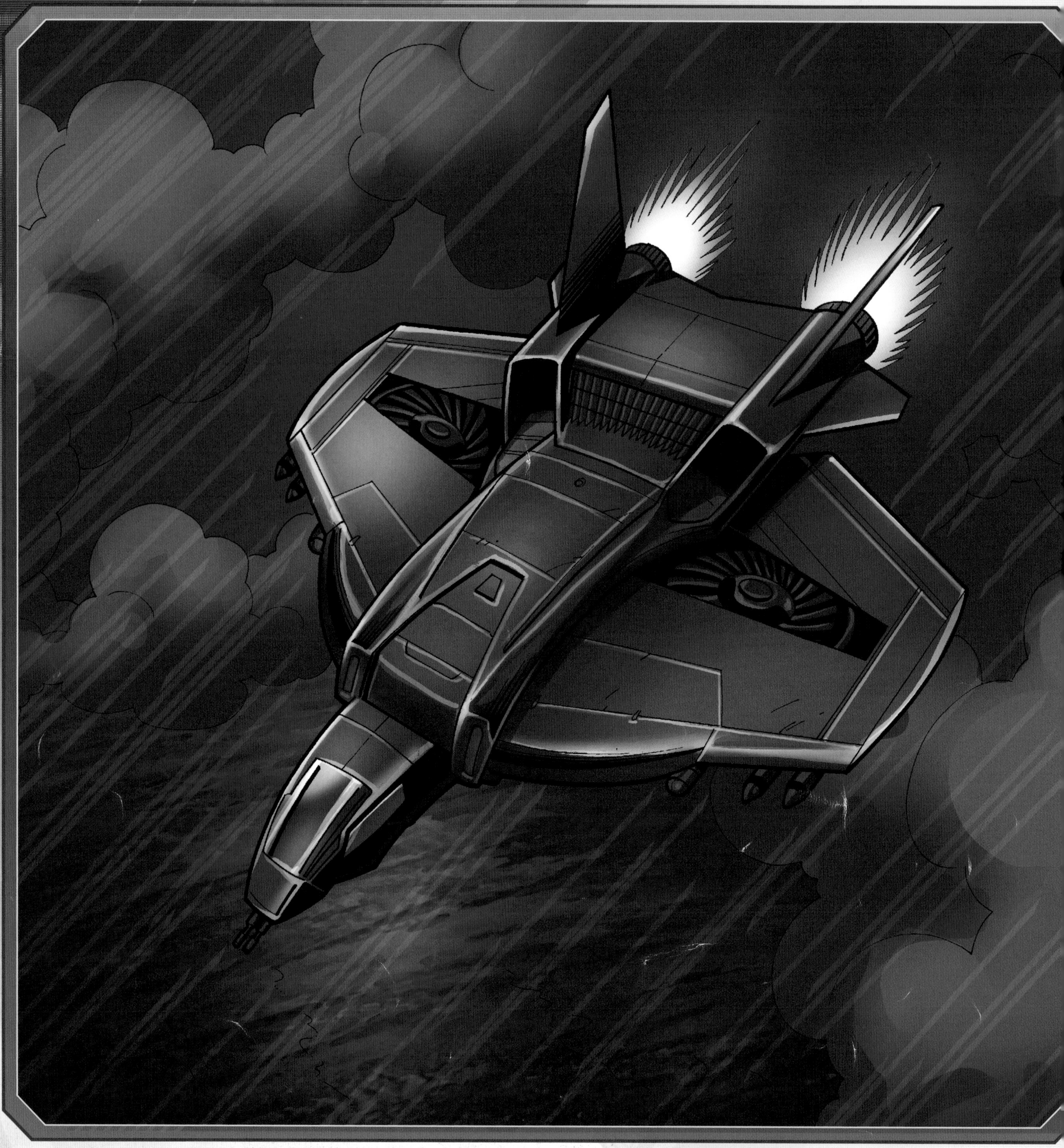

S.H.I.E.L.D. QUINJET

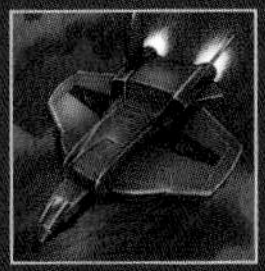

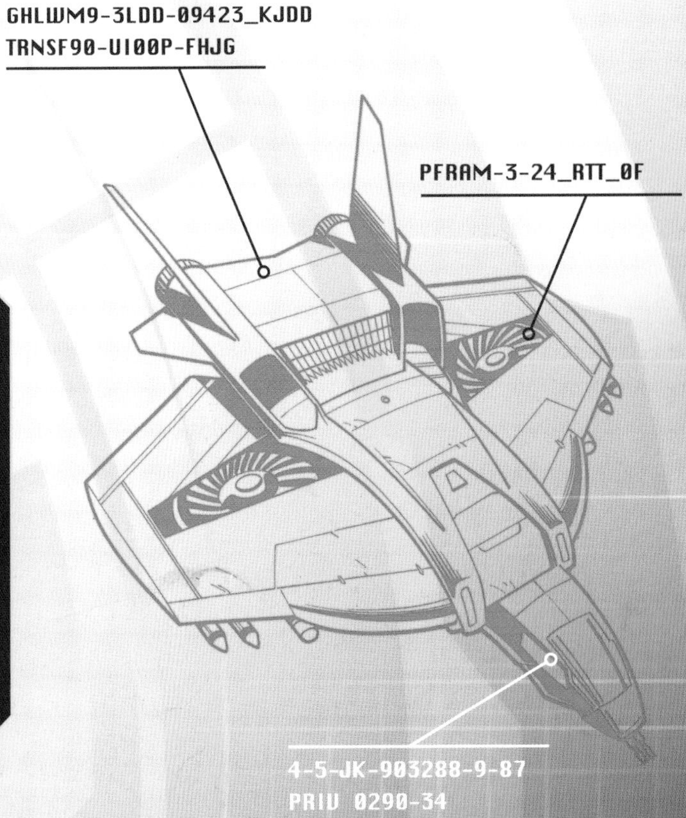

GHLWM9-3LDD-09423_KJDD
TRNSF90-UI00P-FHJG
PFRAM-3-24_RTT_0F
4-5-JK-903288-9-87
PRIV 0290-34

THE QUINJET is a staple in the aerial arsenal used by S.H.I.E.L.D. agents, including the Avengers. Each Quinjet is equipped with turbojet engines and can reach speeds of Mach 2. Equipped with the latest guidance technology, the Quinjet is S.H.I.E.L.D.'s go-to vehicle for transportation into remote or hostile locations.

VIDEO FOOTAGE OF CAPTAIN AMERICA

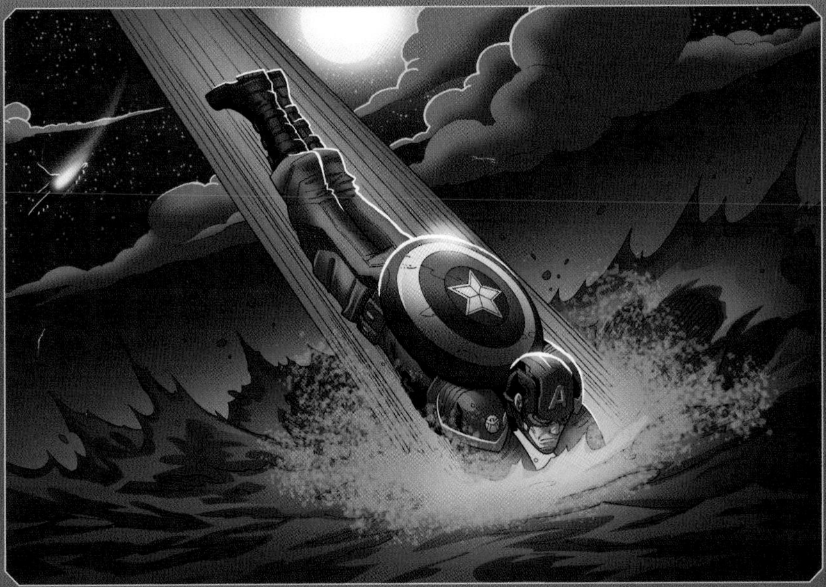

PROPERTY OF
S.H.I.E.L.D.

Recently, the Quinjet transported the special ops team into the Indian Ocean, where they dove out through the back hatch, parachuting safely onto the *Lemurian Star*.

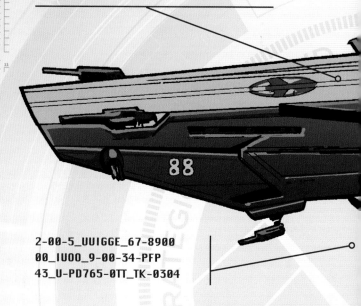

87-34TTG-3039-H_T054-0-45_M90-21
EL056YYJ9923K4-4-34990_L_PARAM2

THE HELICARRIER is a quintessential cornerstone of S.H.I.E.L.D. and the "office" of Fury's mobile operations. It has two stacked carrier decks and optical camouflage capabilities. Recently, three new, advanced models of the Helicarrier were unveiled by Nick Fury to only a select few, including Captain America.

S.H.I.E.L.D. plans to link the Helicarriers to a series of satellites in space. Once the Helicarriers are launched in the air, they will remain there—permanently. They will have continuous flight due to the new repulsor engines provided by Stark Industries. Each contains a targeting hub: a large clear sphere that lives at the front of the Helicarrier. The "unibeam system," as it has been called, can eliminate a thousand individual targets per minute. The tech can read anyone's DNA and will be able to neutralize threats before they even start. In a nutshell, this may reduce operational head counts as fewer S.H.I.E.L.D. agents will be needed in the field.

2-00-5_UUIGGE_67-8900
00_IUOO_9-00-34-PFP
43_U-PD765-0TT_TK-0304

PROJECT INSIGHT:
●ALPHA ●BRAVO ●CHARLIE

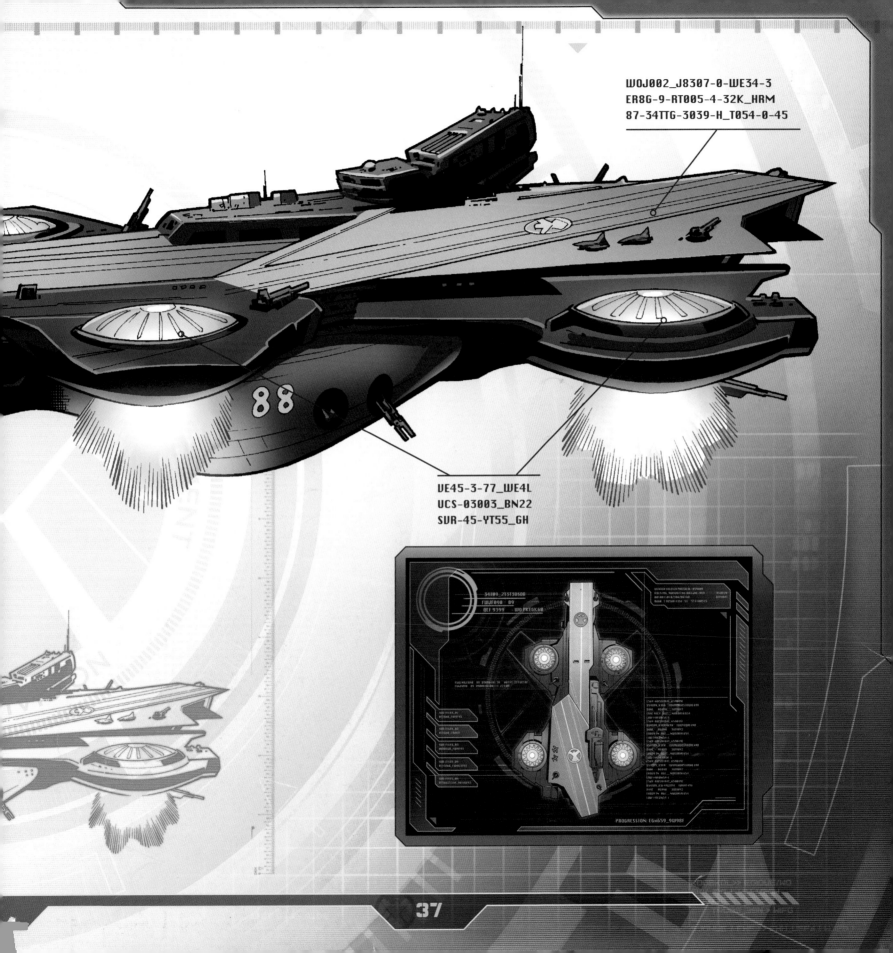

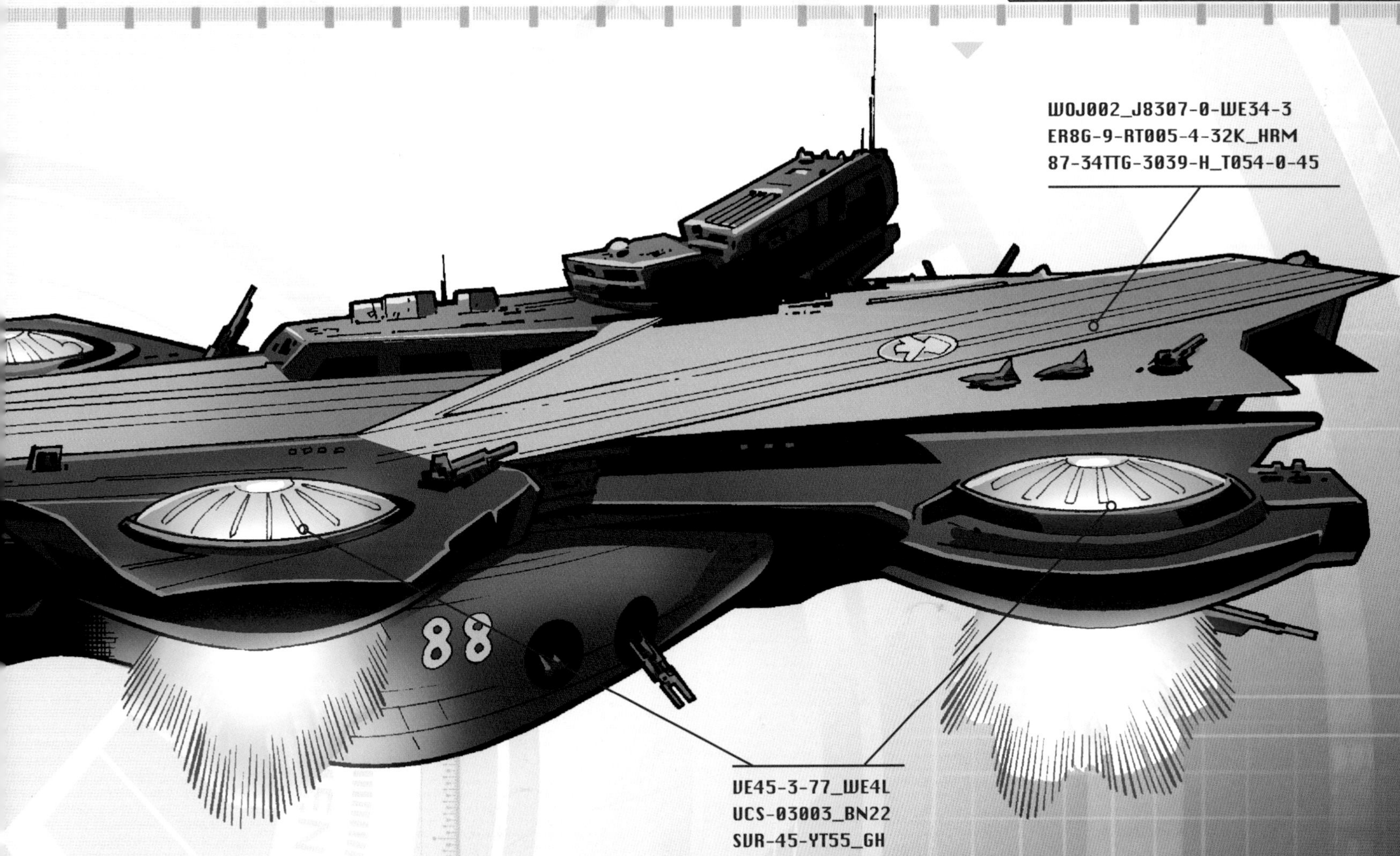
WOJ002_J8307-0-WE34-3
ER8G-9-RT005-4-32K_HRM
87-34TTG-3039-H_T054-0-45
VE45-3-77_WE4L
UCS-03003_BN22
SVR-45-YT55_GH

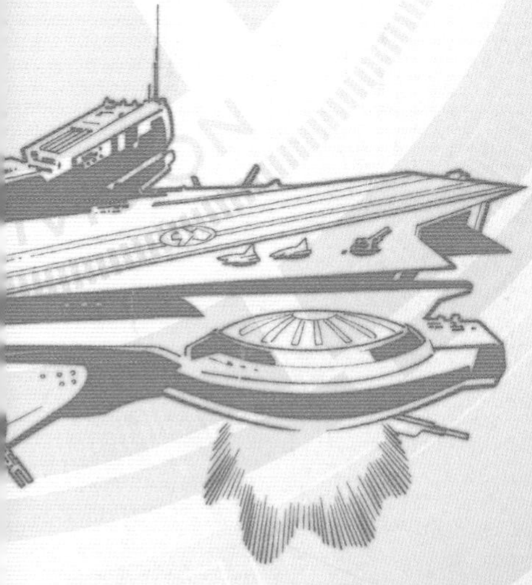

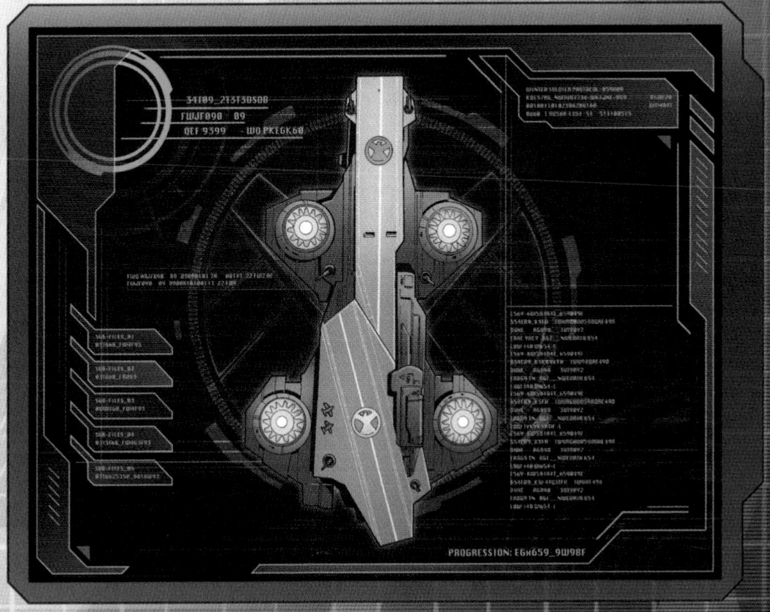

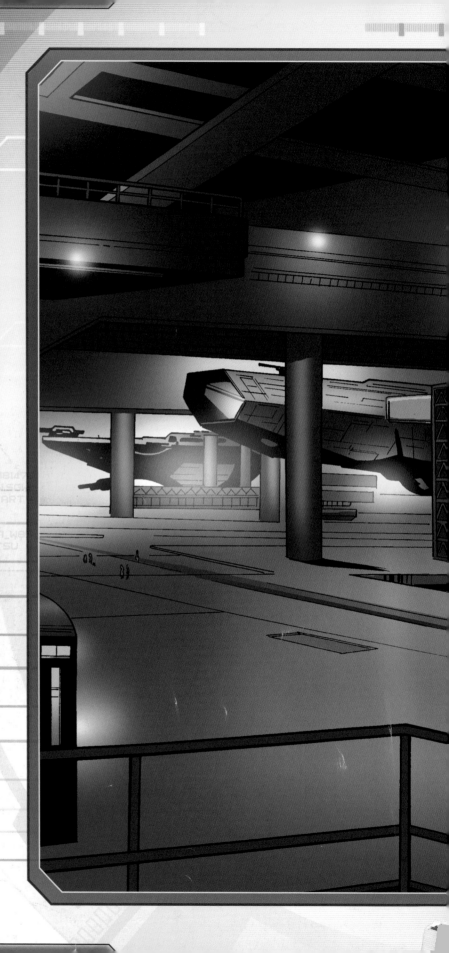

KDGBKDL>> EGIGUE/WO
SKKJDGJ...WIWJ,GIGH
>> KDJA
    TRUOS_39N > WIFG

SJGHUE / FHF >> FHH_UEF4 [WJFB]

N _1181478
KJW.SGWI - WGIS35
VD   ART - 83

G - ATI_W85U
2T96TSU

VE3_17887RHY

KDGBKDL>> EGIGUE/WO
SKKJDGJ...WIWJ,GIGH
>> KDJA
    TRUOS_39N > WIFG

SJGHUE / FHF >> FHH

439T 9 WII - ALGE

Beneath the Triskelion lie the newer versions of the Helicarrier.

Their code names are **ALPHA**, **BRAVO**, and **CHARLIE**.

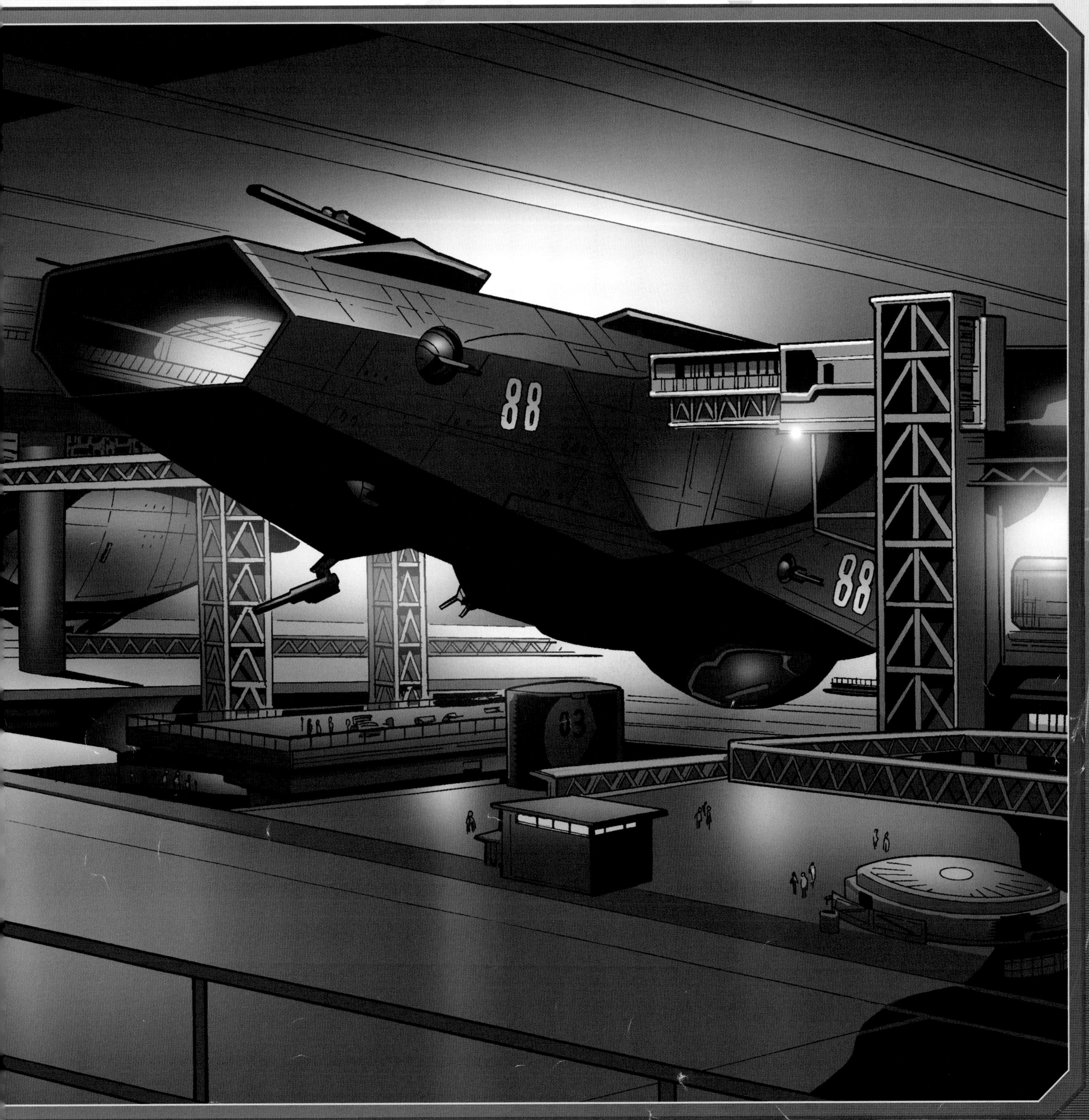
88
88
03

BATTERING RAM

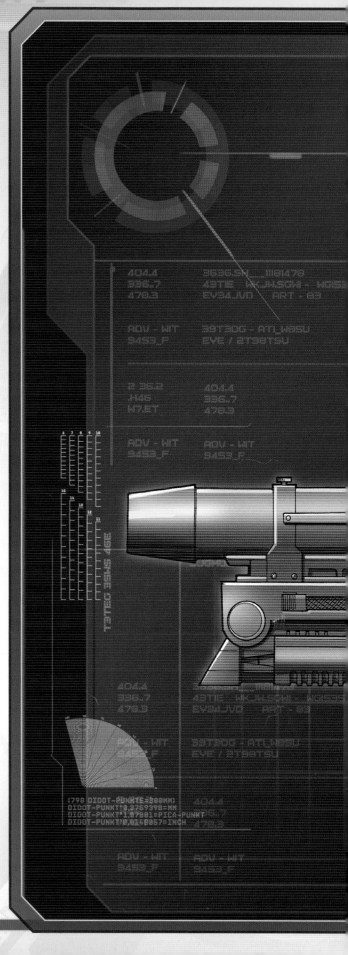

DEPLOYED during the street battle with Fury's SUV, the battering ram anchored to the asphalt and began to power up, creating an intense energy hum that finally unleashed a menacing impact against the vehicle. After several "rams," the vehicle's defense systems unexpectedly failed and the impenetrable windshield became penetrable. We have never seen technology like this and, for the record, are not sure why. We would love to get our hands on the blueprints and perhaps replicate its design. Agent ▬▬▬▬▬▬ is tracking the origin of the battering ram. More information to come.

S.H.I.E.L.D.

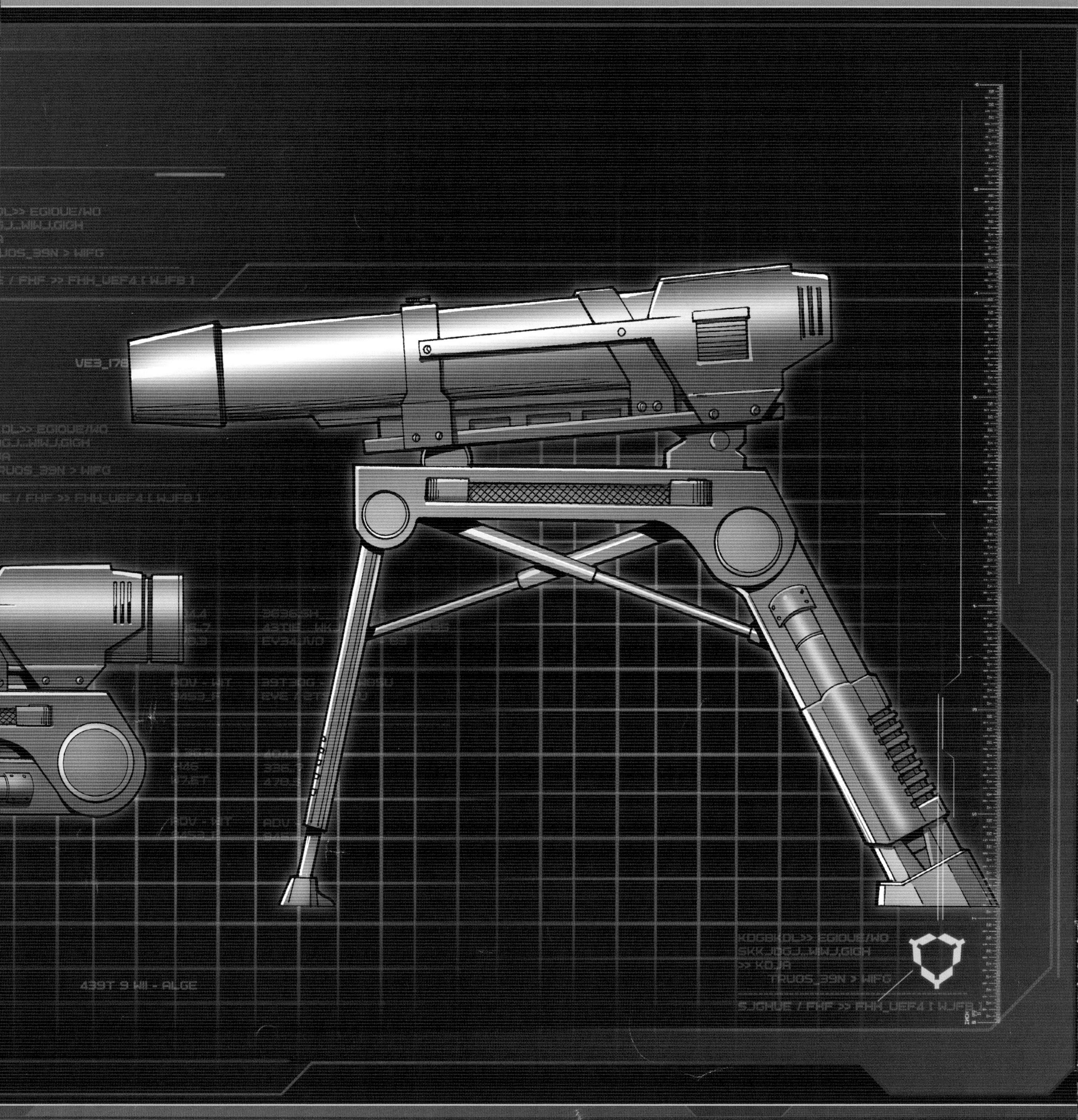

OL>> EGIOUE/WO
J_WIW_J.GIOH
UOS_39N > WIFG
/ FHF >> FHH_UEF4 I WJFB 1

VE3_I78

OL>> EGIOUE/WO
..HIWJ.GIOH
RUOS_39N > WIFG
E / FHF >> FHH_UEF4 I WJFB 1

439T 9 WII - ALGE

KOGBKOL>> EGIOUE/WO
SKK JOGJ_WIW_J.GIOH
>> KOJA
TRUOS_39N > WIFG

SJOHUE / FHF >> FHH_UEF4 I WJFB

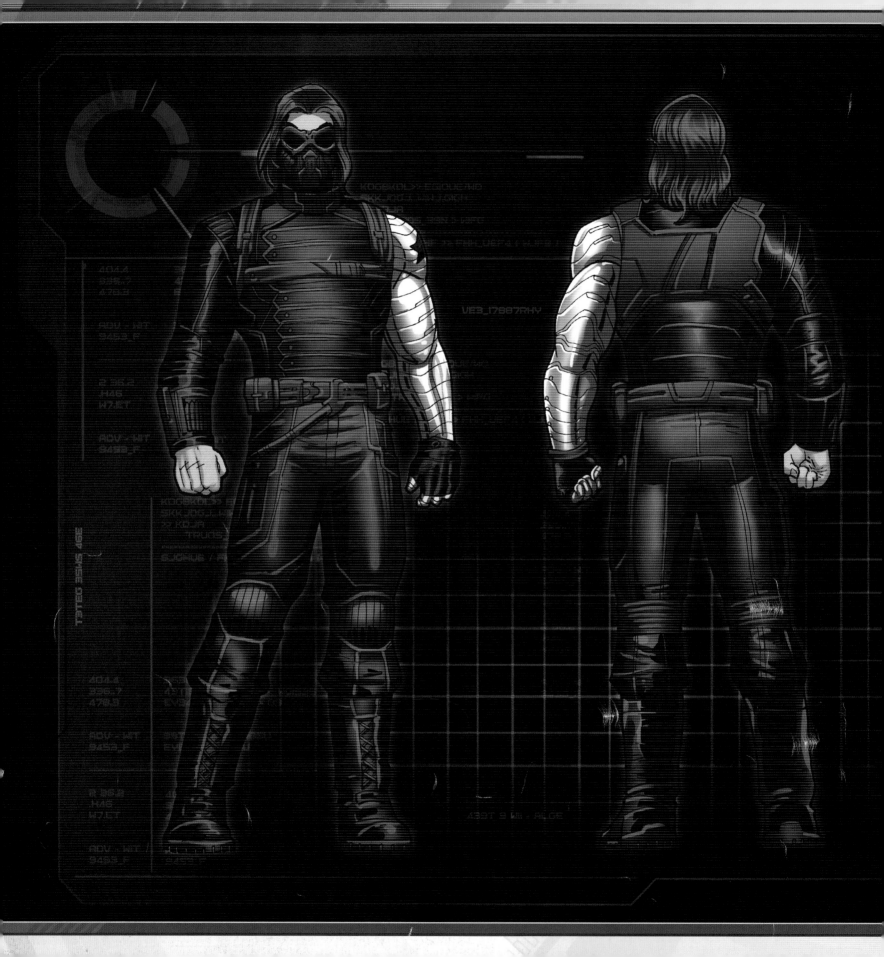

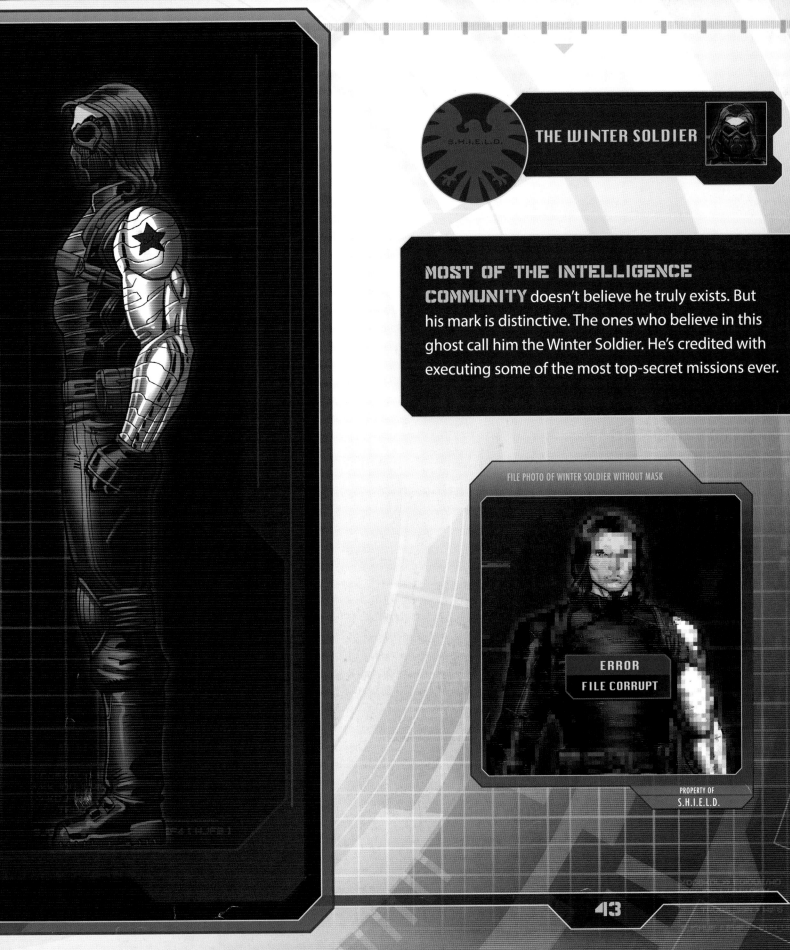

THE WINTER SOLDIER

MOST OF THE INTELLIGENCE COMMUNITY doesn't believe he truly exists. But his mark is distinctive. The ones who believe in this ghost call him the Winter Soldier. He's credited with executing some of the most top-secret missions ever.

FILE PHOTO OF WINTER SOLDIER WITHOUT MASK

ERROR
FILE CORRUPT

PROPERTY OF
S.H.I.E.L.D.

THE WINTER SOLDIER

THE MYSTERY of Captain America's latest and most frightening adversary, the Winter Soldier, has confounded the intelligence community for more than fifty years. By all accounts the unidentified agent is a myth, applying his infamous skill set at the crossroads of history and conspiracy and then disappearing into the cold without a trace.

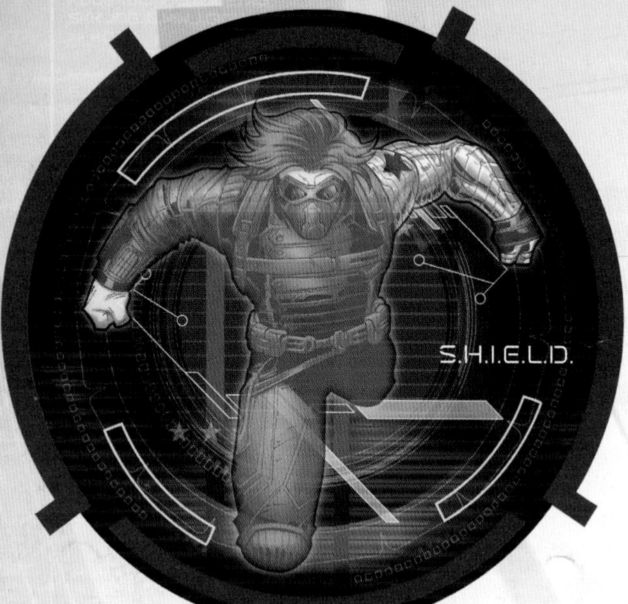
S.H.I.E.L.D.

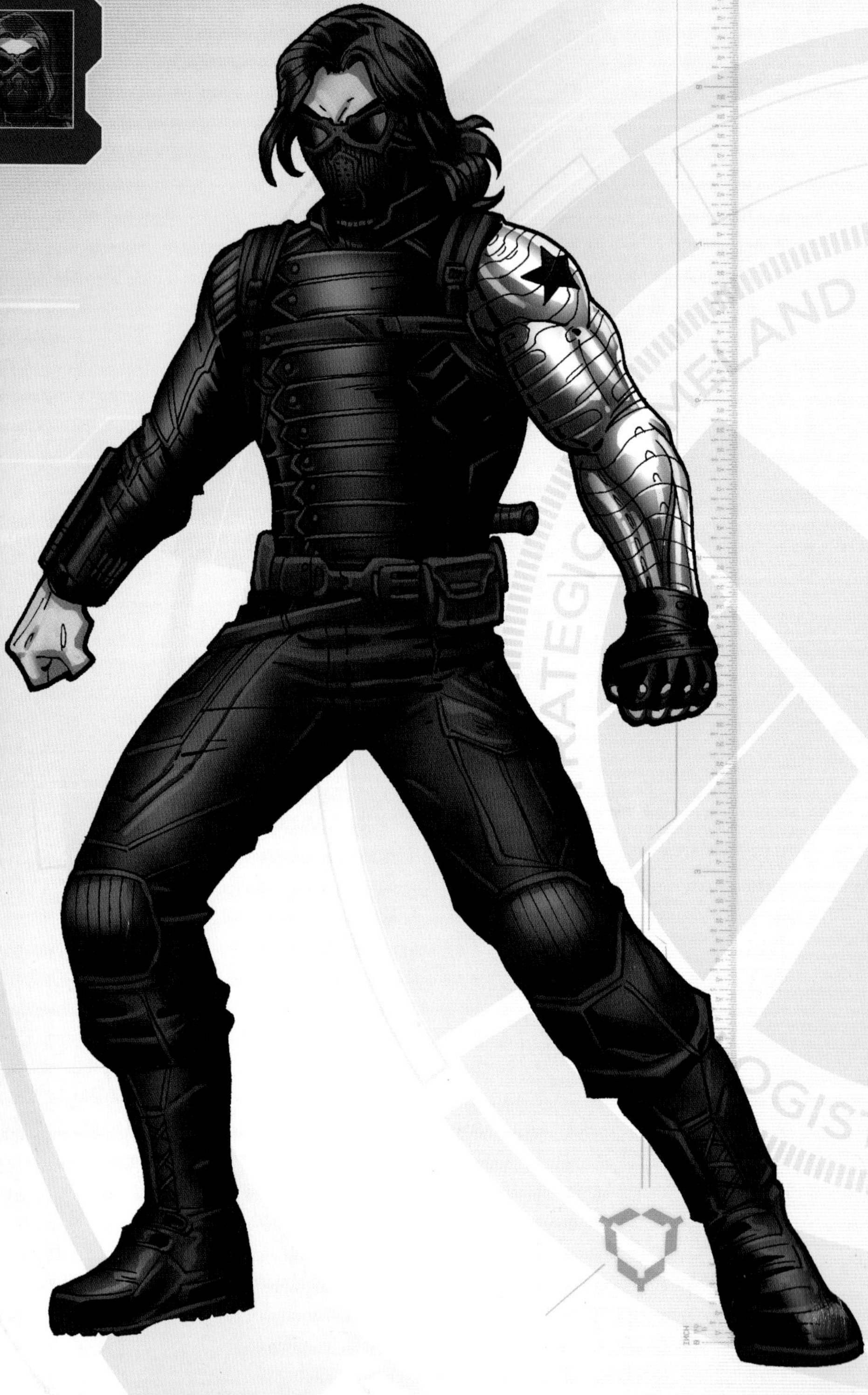

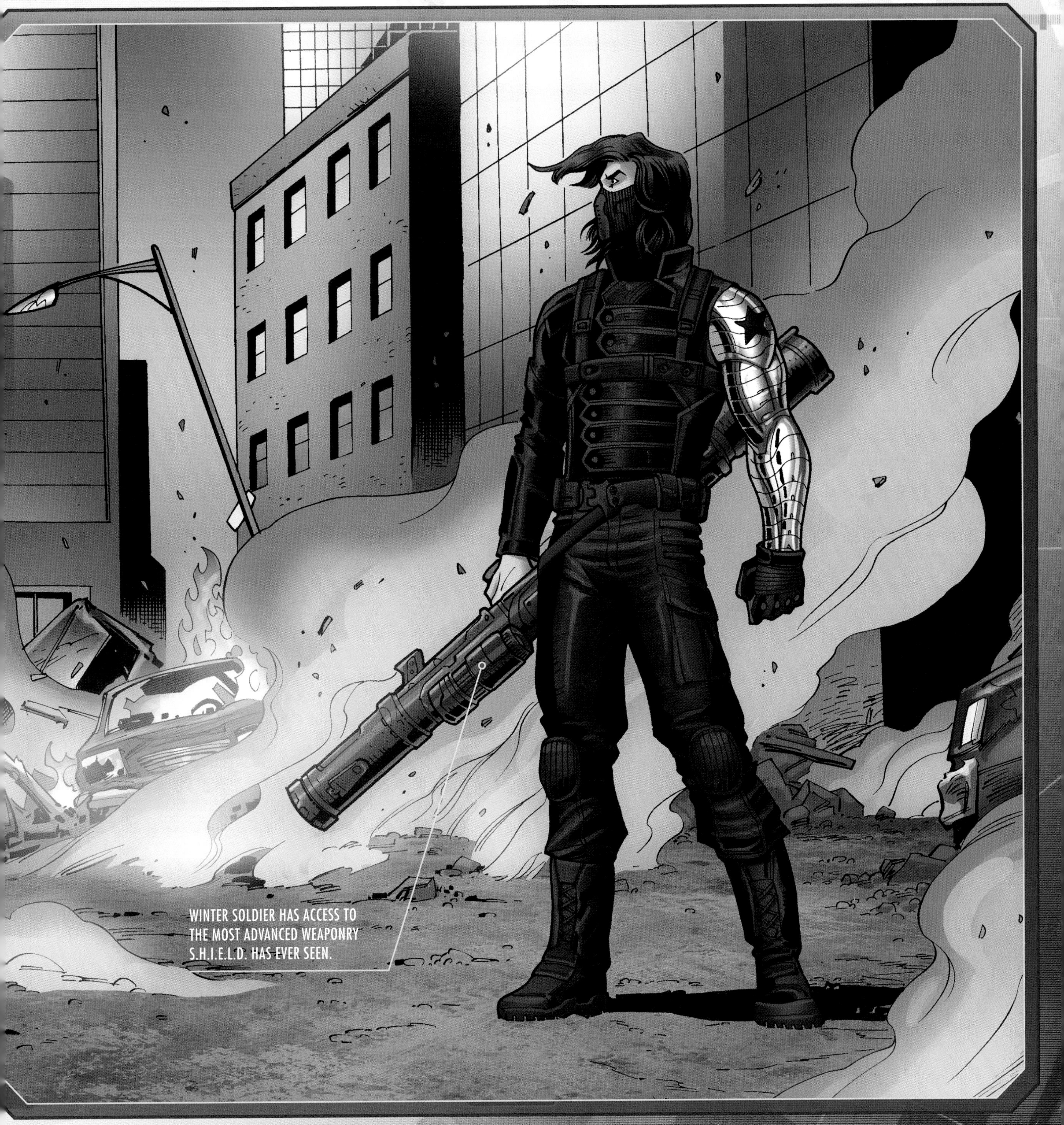
WINTER SOLDIER HAS ACCESS TO THE MOST ADVANCED WEAPONRY S.H.I.E.L.D. HAS EVER SEEN.

THE WINTER SOLDIER

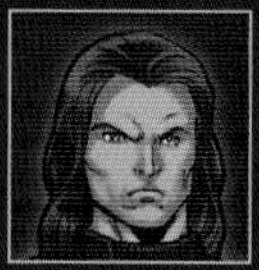

JAMES BUCHANAN BARNES was a childhood friend of Steve Rogers. Both born in Brooklyn, "Bucky" (his nickname) and Steve grew up on the streets of Williamsburg, Brooklyn, playing stickball and marbles. Bucky and Steve were inseparable both in the schoolyard and later on the battlefield. When Steve Rogers became Captain America, he and Bucky, along with his fellow Howling Commandos, battled across Europe in search of HYDRA. Tragically, Bucky perished while on a secret mission with Captain America. Steve took full responsibility for his best friend's death and never forgave himself for it. To make matters worse, Bucky's body was never found and Steve was never able to give his dear friend a proper burial.

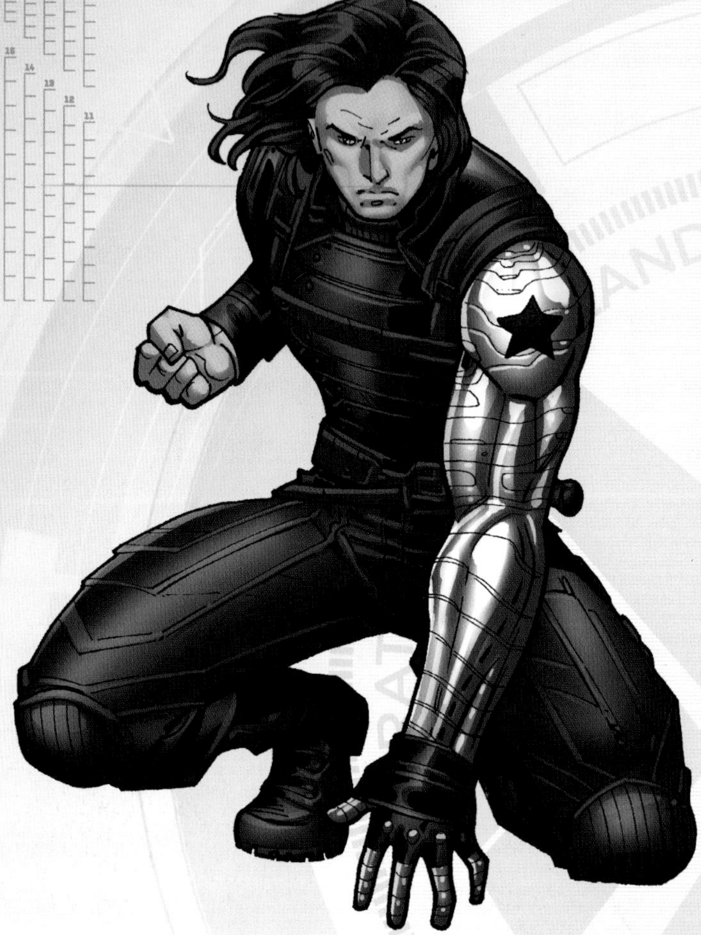

FILE PHOTO OF CODE NAME: WINTER SOLDIER

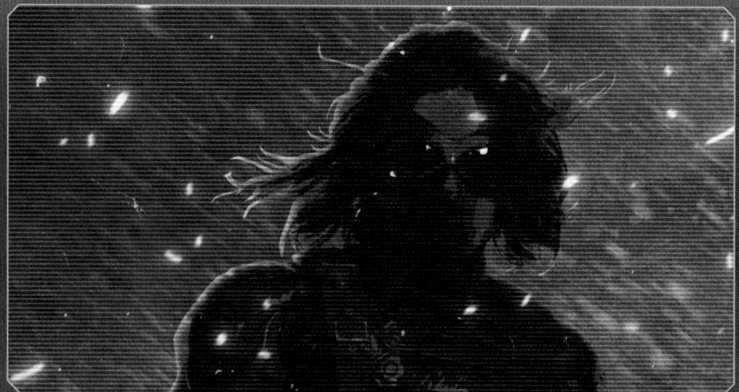

PROPERTY OF S.H.I.E.L.D.

Recent reports have come in about the sudden appearance of James Buchanan Barnes. Local surveillance cameras in downtown D.C. provided the images.

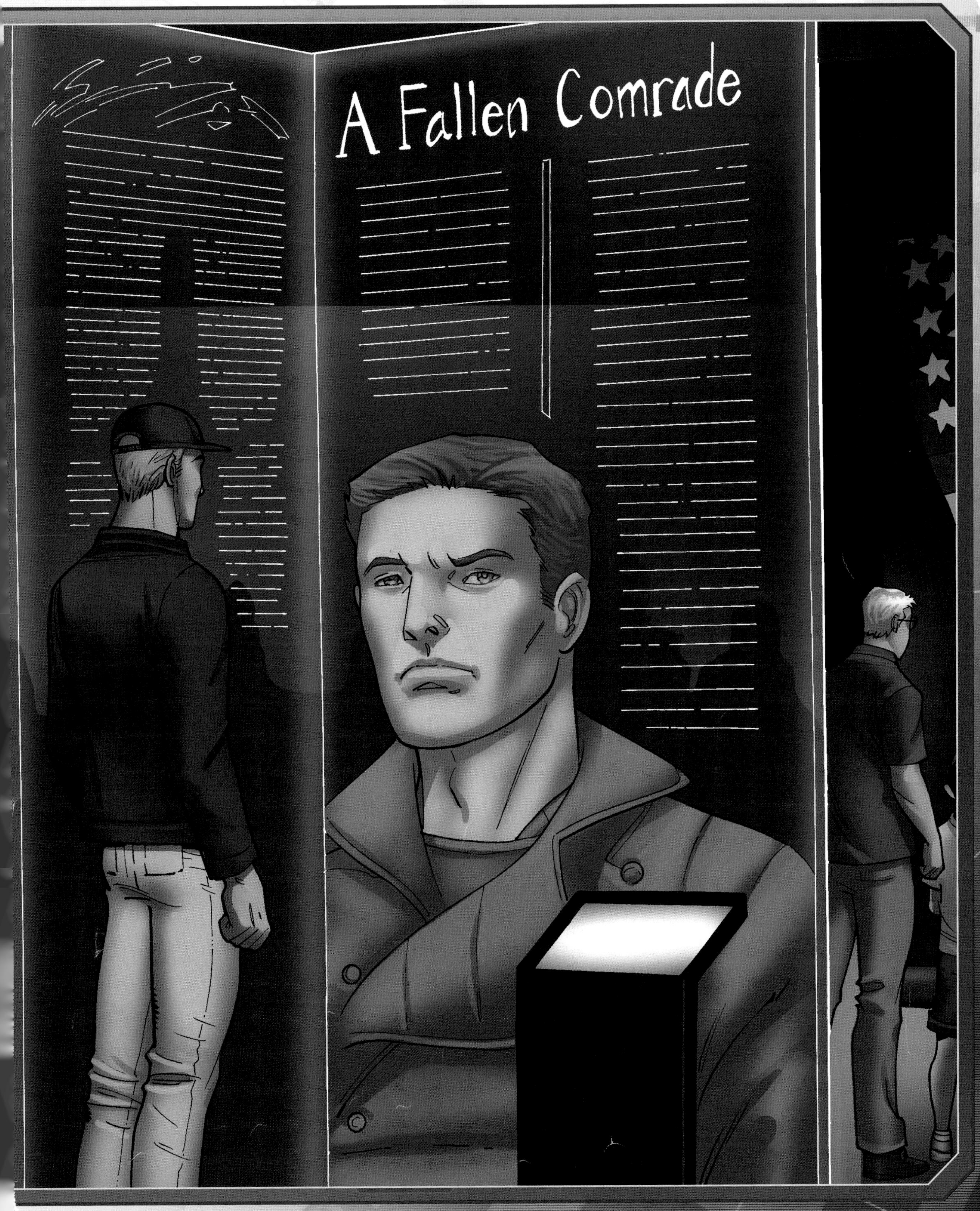
A Fallen Comrade

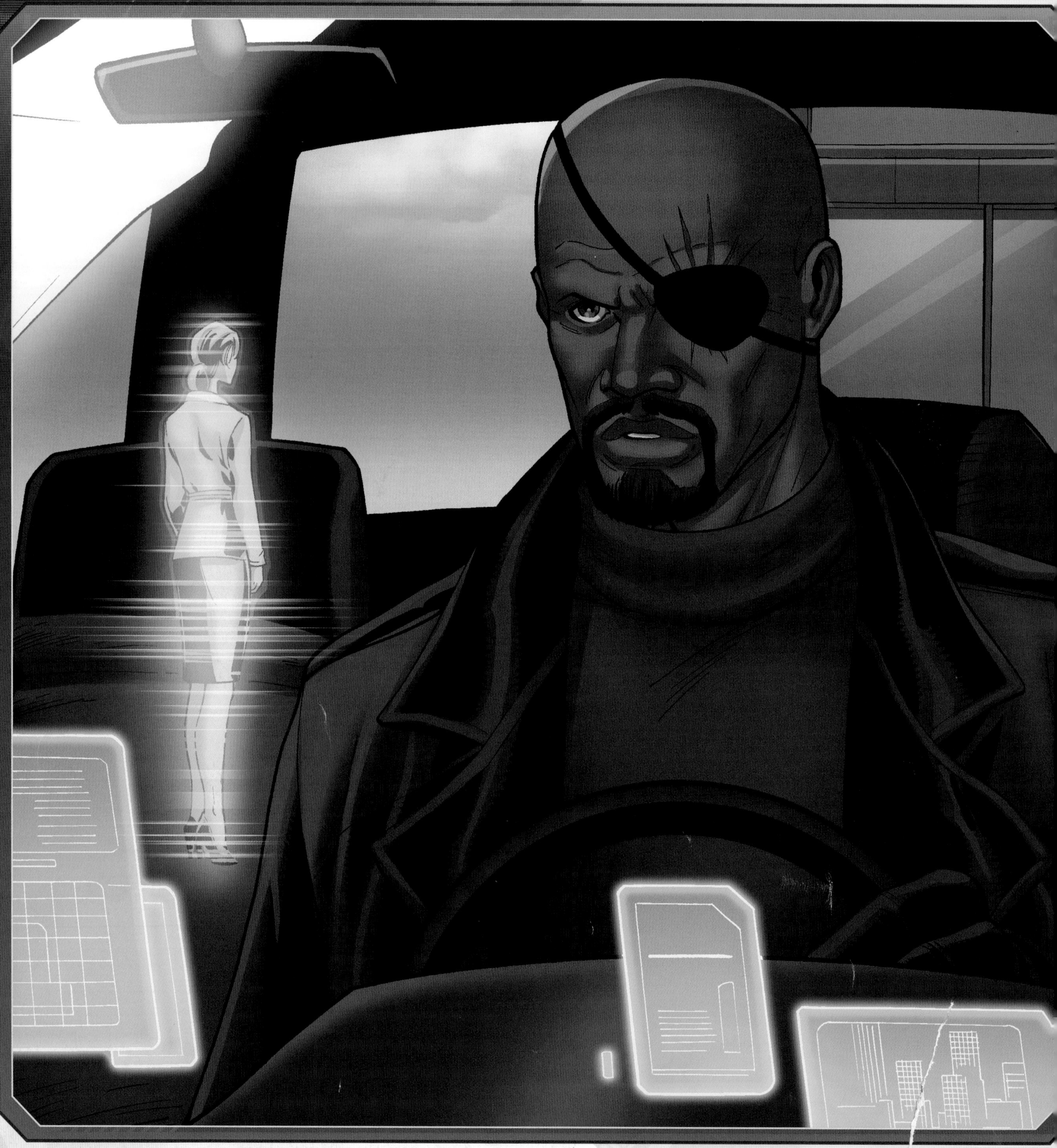

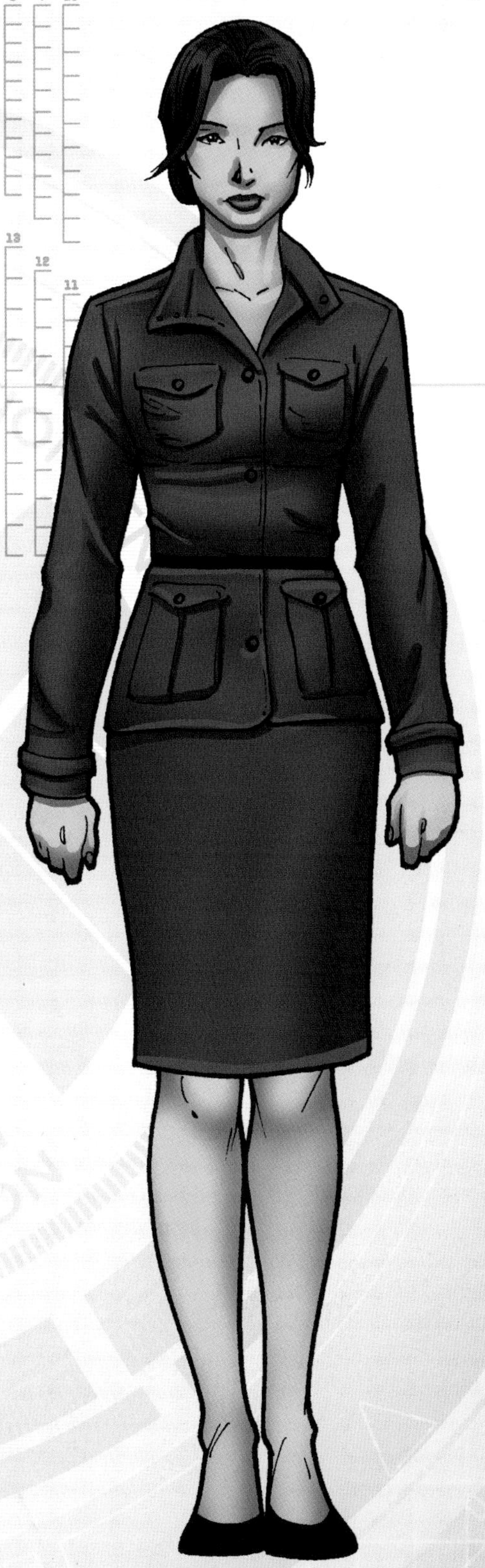

MARIA HILL

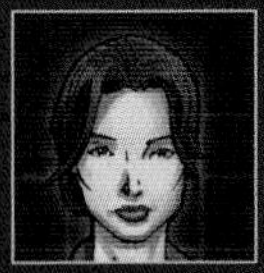

MARIA HILL is Nick Fury's second-in-command and has been by his side since the Avengers initiative began. When specific intel is needed, Maria answers the call. She is available to Nick Fury whenever he needs her. With the S.H.I.E.L.D. mainframe at her fingertips, she is able to answer any question in seconds. But her talents go beyond mining data. Maria is a highly skilled fighter and weapons expert who on occasion joins the team out in the field. When Loki first appeared on Earth, it was at a remote S.H.I.EL.D. subbase facility located at [redacted]. When the Tesseract, in the care of one Dr. Erik Selvig, opened a wormhole to another dimension, out stepped Loki and a brutal skirmish ensued. Maria Hill quickly jumped into action and went after Loki through the tunnels of the substation. Unfortunately, Loki escaped, but Maria's dedication to her work and her team proves to be a great asset.

WITH S.H.I.E.L.D. AGENT MARIA HILL on secure line 0405, Nick Fury ordered her to D.C. for further briefing on the hostage situation on the *Lemurian Star*. That was the last communication we had with Fury before he was attacked by falsely marked Washington, D.C., police cars. Satellite photos obtained from [redacted] display Fury being blocked in and rammed from three angles by these unknown attackers. Thanks to his state-of-the-art S.H.I.E.L.D. assault vehicle, Fury was able to survive the first wave of attacks.

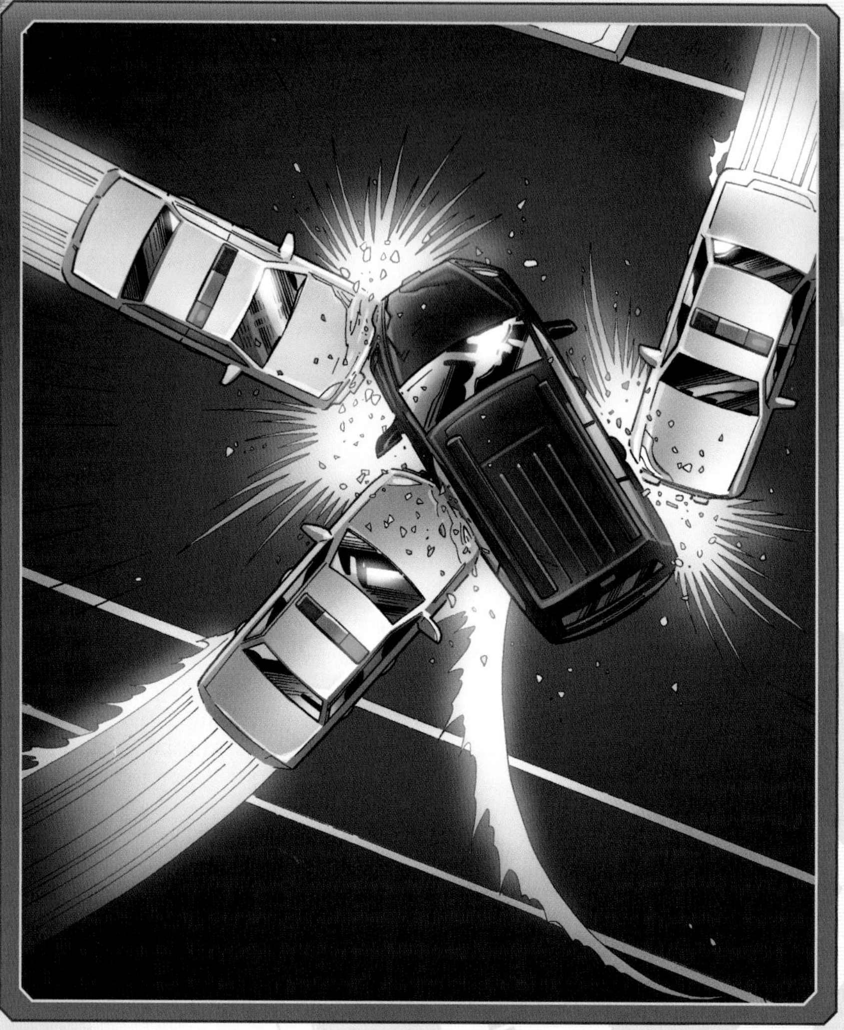

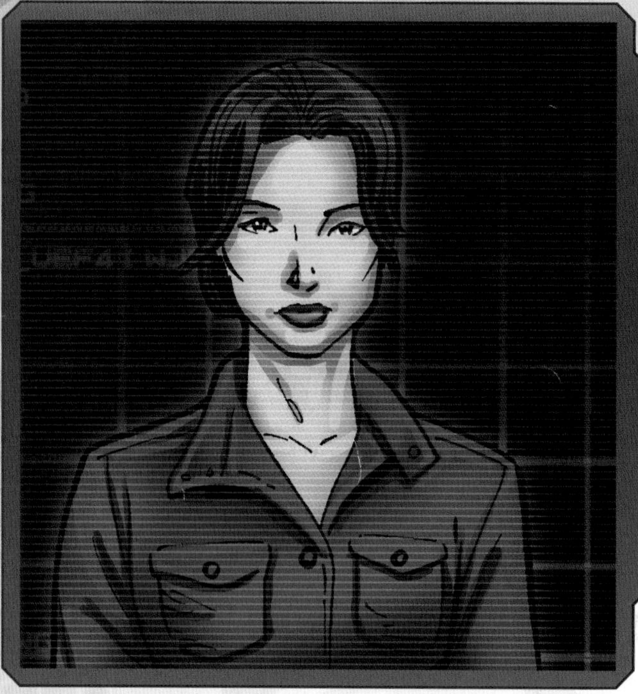

A digital facial scan was initiated on the attackers. Reports came back that they were unknown assailants. With S.H.I.E.L.D.'s data bank registering almost every single person on the planet, we are unsure how these results came back as unknown. Agent [redacted] is looking into this more.

Reports indicate the shell integrity of the vehicle was severely damaged by a high-tech and unknown device we have labeled "THE RAM" for reporting purposes. The picture in this file shows the immense strength the device had against our S.H.I.E.L.D. vehicle. The technology is reportedly top of the line and rivals that of Stark Industries. The device has been recovered from the scene and sent off for analysis. Failure became imminent and countermeasures were enabled so that Fury could turn the tables on his unknown assailants and halt their attack. Fury then demanded that the guidance cameras activate as he grabbed the wheel. Cameras displayed alternate angles of the car's rear, side, and front views. Fury weaved through the traffic, navigating by the screens, and made a narrow and dangerous escape.

That is, until the computer informed Fury that an incoming projectile had been detected. Digital video displays a masked man with a high-tech launcher standing in the middle of the road. The assassin fired, and based on our heat sensor readings taken from the vehicle, a black disk slid into the street. This is where the data stopped relaying. Reports show that the vehicle was hit by the disk and flipped on its roof. CCTV shows a strange masked man approaching the vehicle and finding it— empty. Fury has yet to be located.

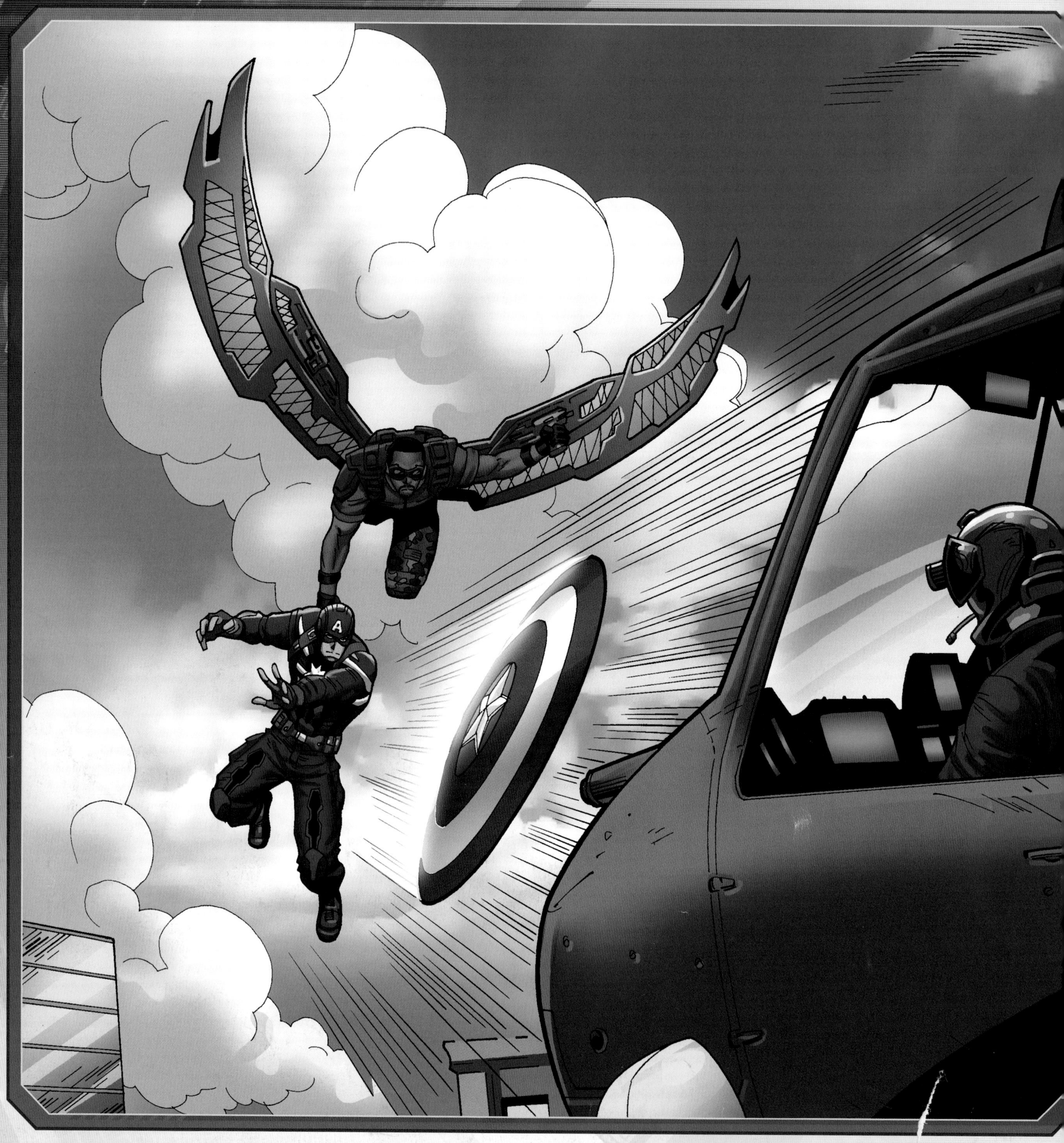

THE BATTLE OF CAPTAIN AMERICA AND THE WINTER SOLDIER

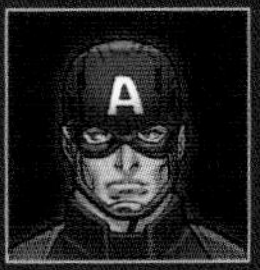

A brief fight occurred with the Winter Soldier getting the upper hand, tossing Cap from the chopper to the streets below, where he smashed into a local school bus!

FROM THE STREETS OF DOWNTOWN WASHINGTON, D.C., TO THE SKIES ABOVE IT, the battle between Captain America and the Winter Soldier unfolded before hundreds of eyewitnesses. Several high-tech choppers buzzed overhead and within one of the choppers was the mysterious Winter Soldier. At one point, the battle took to the sky with the aid of Sam Wilson—in his EXO-7 Falcon wings—who hoisted Captain America up from the street.

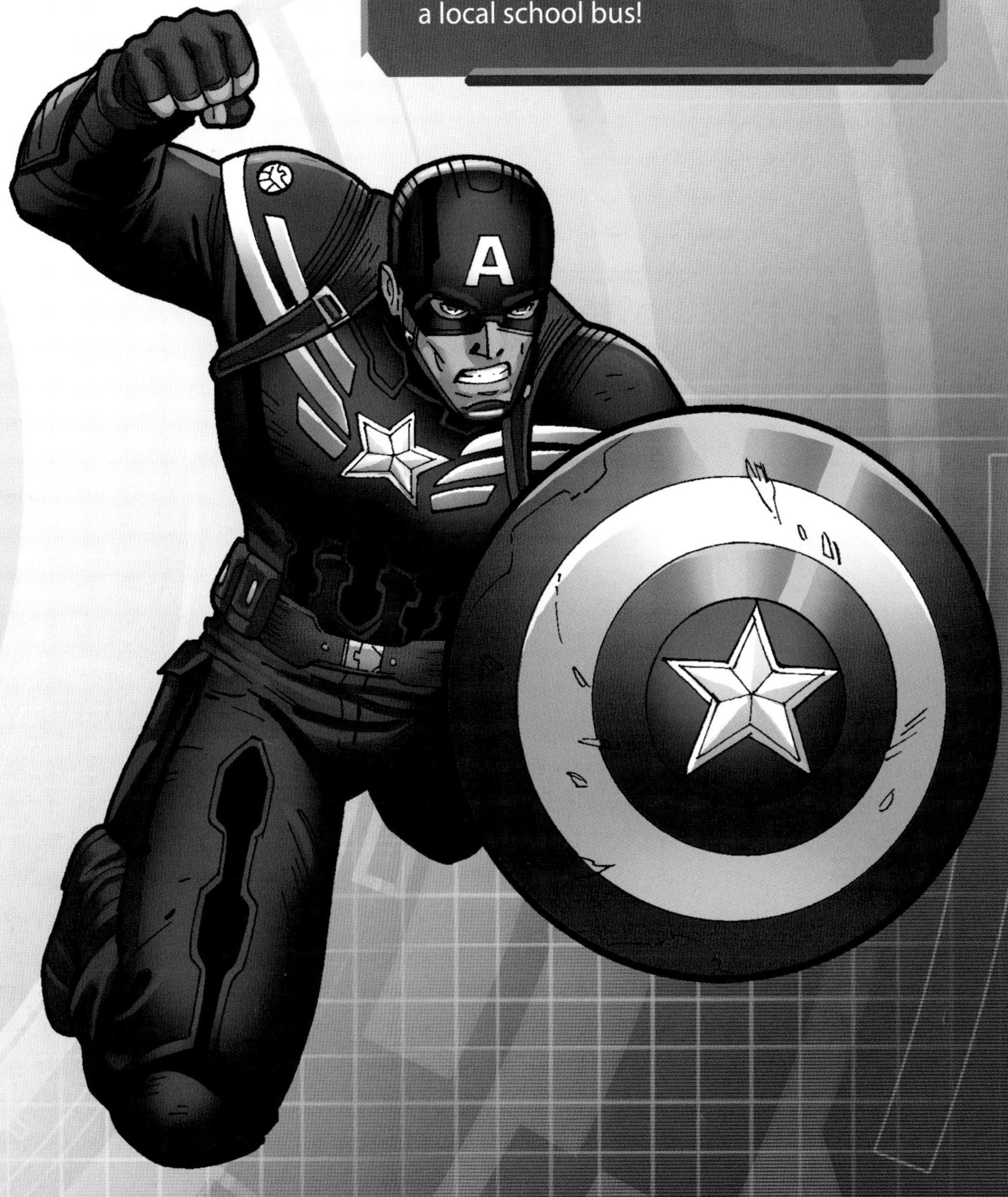
A

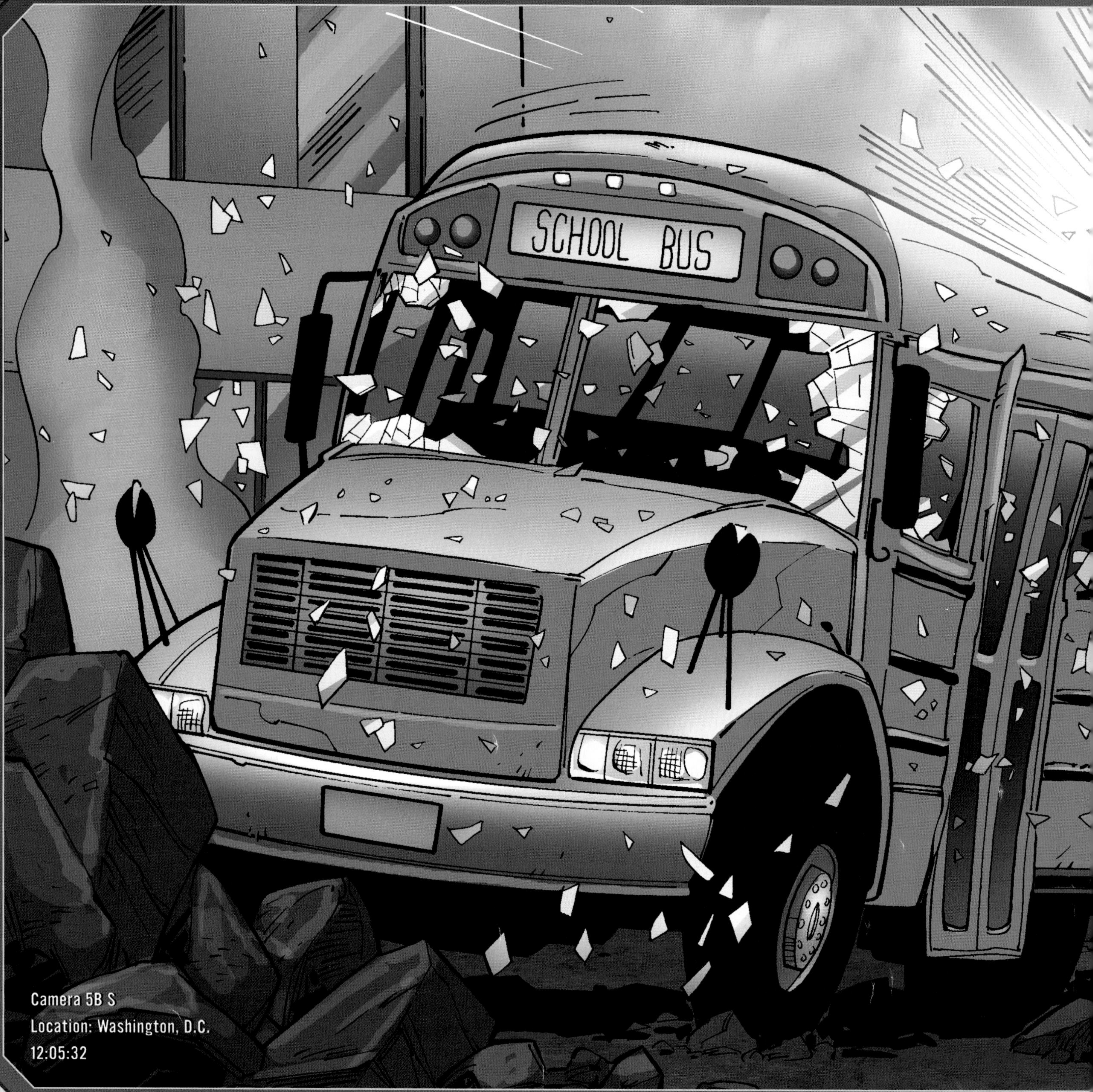
SCHOOL BUS
Camera 5B S
Location: Washington, D.C.
12:05:32

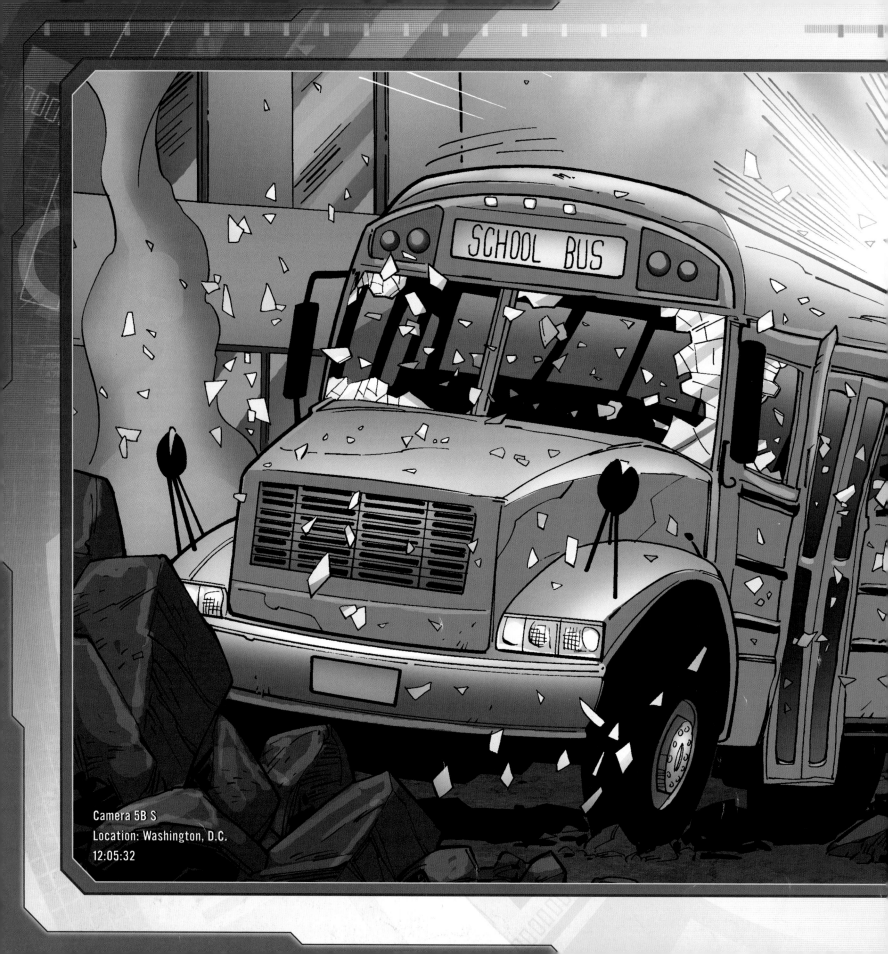

Thanks to Cap's **SUPER-SOLDIER SERUM**, he was able to survive this fall.

(798 DIDOT-PUNKTE=300MM)
DIDOT-PUNKT*0.3759398=MM
DIDOT-PUNKT*1.07001=PICA-PUNKT
DIDOT-PUNKT*0.0148057=INCH

WHILE CAPTAIN AMERICA WAS DOWN, Falcon swooped in and handled several of the Winter Soldier's goons—as well as encountering the Winter Soldier himself! Falcon, with his EXO-7 wingsuit, attacked the assassin with precision. At one point during the battle, Falcon grappled with the Winter Soldier and even took the fight to the sky.

VIDEO FOOTAGE OF FALCON

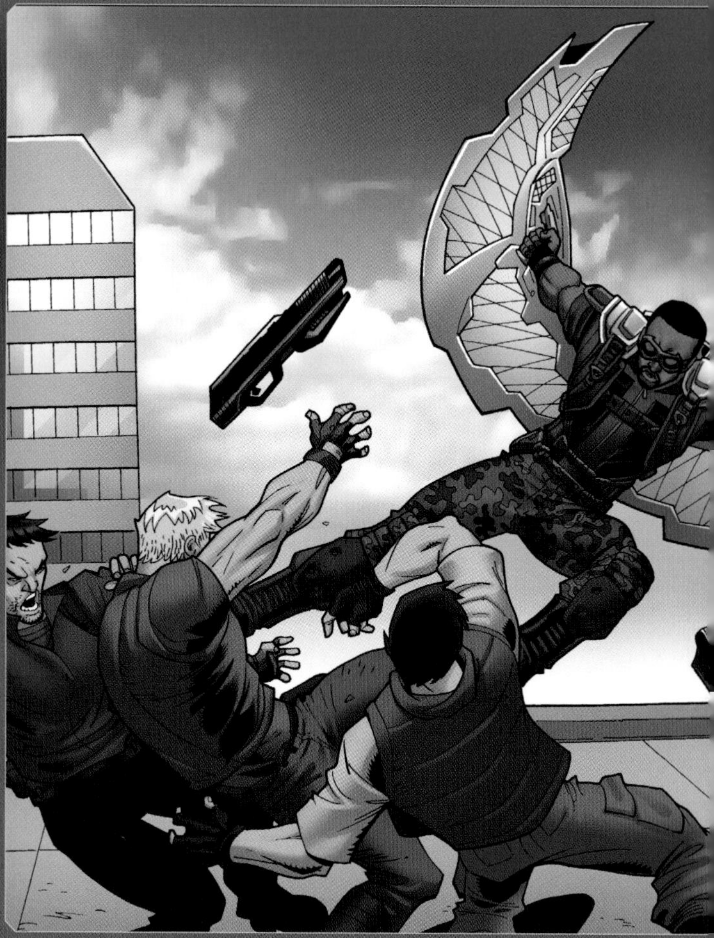

VIDEO OF FALCON AND WINTER SOLDIER

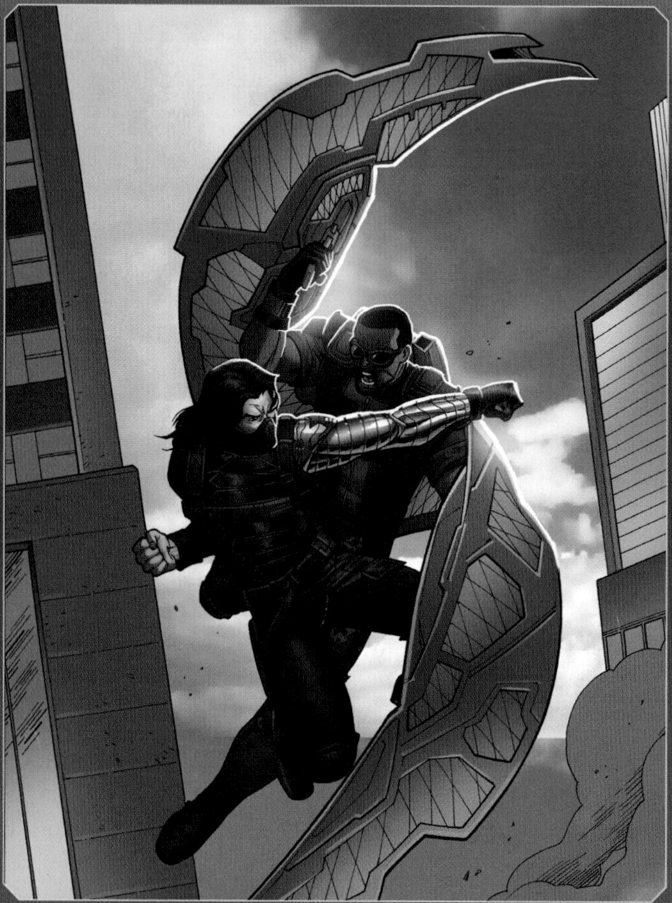

PROPERTY OF
S.H.I.E.L.D.

The Winter Soldier broke free and landed back on the ground, where he turned his attention to Black Widow. Realizing that she was able to tend to her threats alone, Falcon saw an opportunity to take out a few more mercenaries (see file photo taken from a local news helicopter flying in the area).

PROPERTY OF
S.H.I.E.L.D.

FALCON IN ACTION

He dove down in front of one of the choppers, causing the pilot to lose control and crash to the ground. With the sky clear of danger, Falcon focused on the enemies below, disarming them (see photo).

VIDEO FOOTAGE OF FALCON

PROPERTY OF
S.H.I.E.L.D.

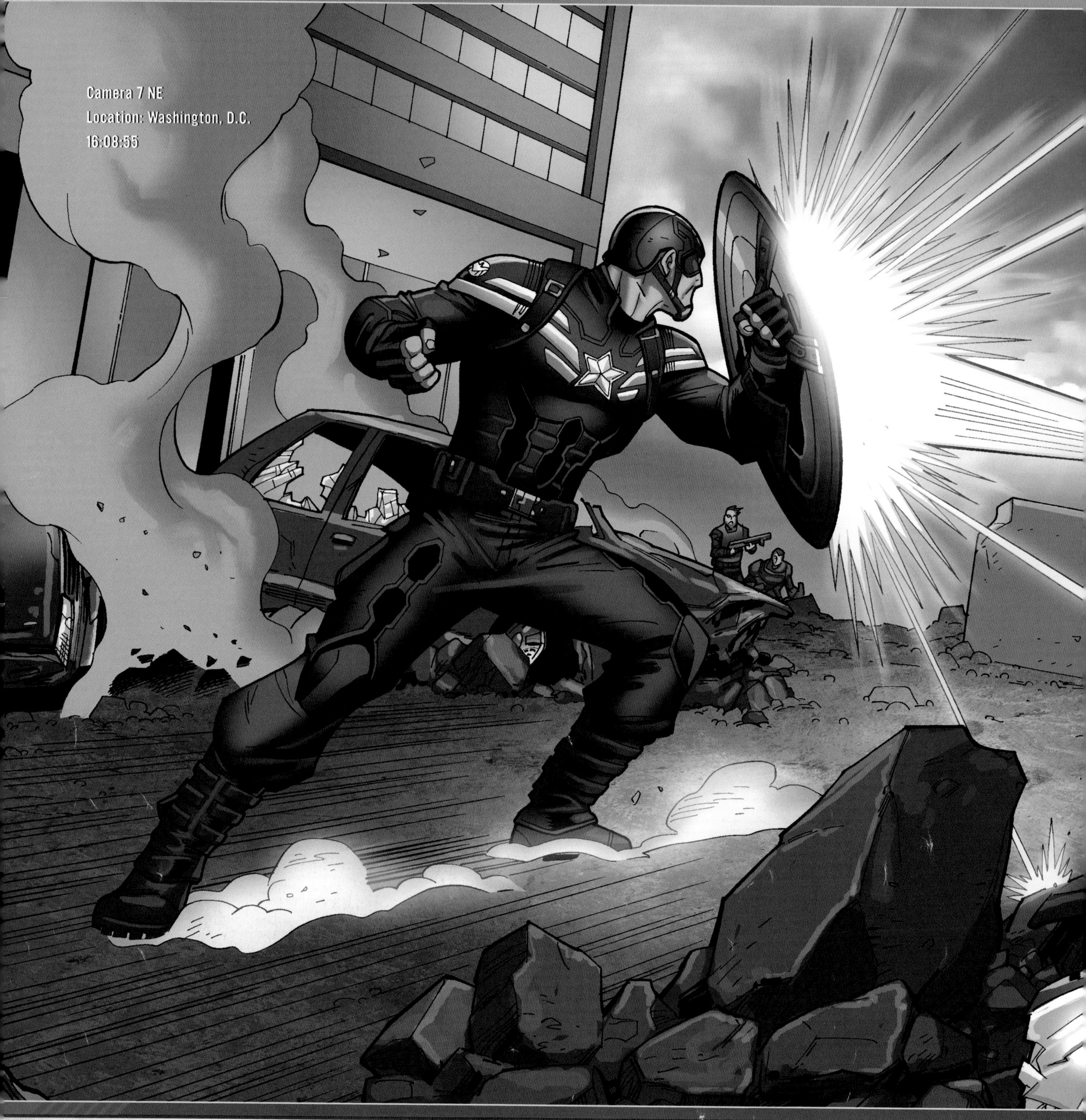
Camera 7 NE
Location: Washington, D.C.
16:08:55

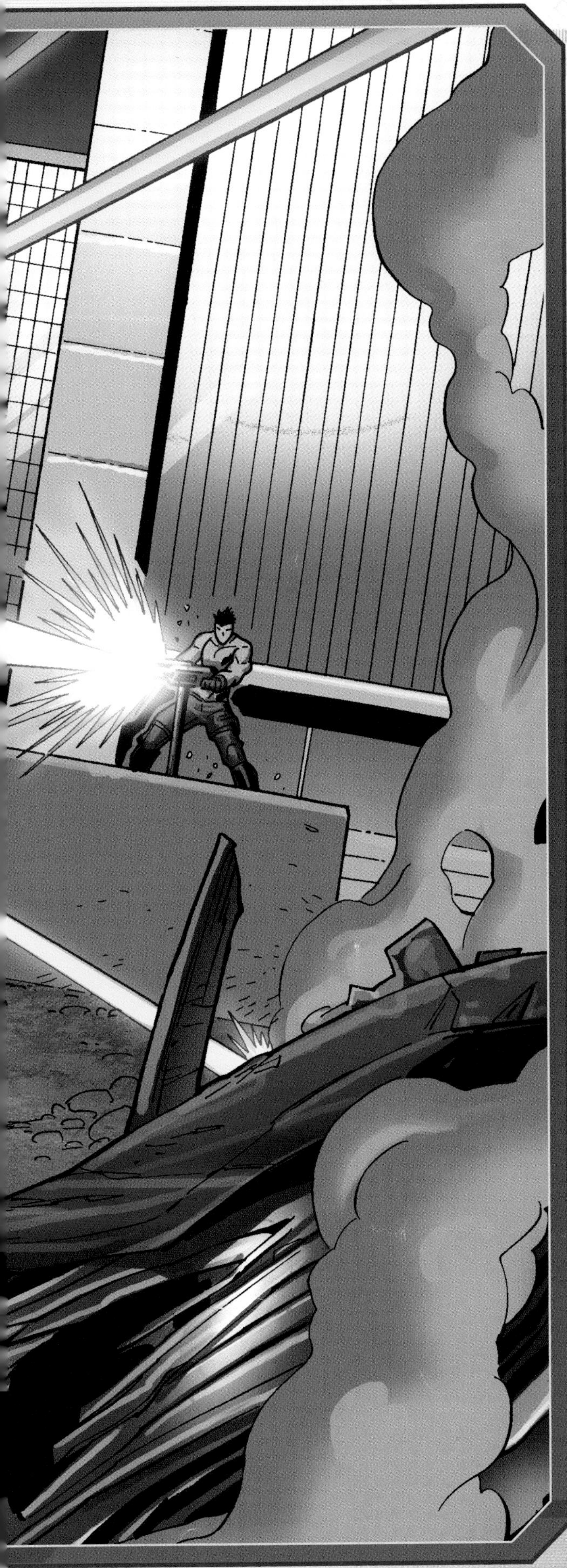

CAPTAIN AMERICA VS. THE GATLING GUN

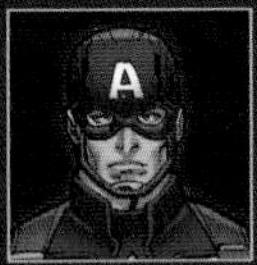

WITHOUT HIS SHIELD, Captain America had to think fast. Outside, several of the Winter Soldier's mercs had set up a high-powered Gatling gun and aimed it at Cap. They fired on the bus that Cap was in, thousands of rounds shredding the exterior. Cap leaped from the bus and dove toward his shield, which lay a few feet away. Eventually he was able to grab it and he moved in on the Gatling gun shooter. The power of the gun pushed back the Super-Soldier, but due to his Vibranium shield, he was able to absorb some of the impact and move forward, eventually reaching the merc and taking him out with a mighty blow.

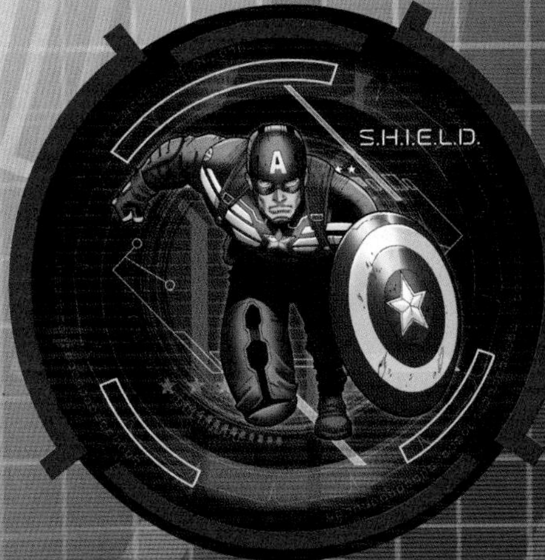
S.H.I.E.L.D.

AFTER AN INTENSE AND FIERCE SHOWDOWN between the Winter Soldier and Captain America, during which several downtown city blocks of D.C. were badly damaged, the two men came to a halt when the Winter Soldier's mask came off, revealing him as Bucky Barnes. Captain America, taken aback, tried to talk to his former best friend. But the Winter Soldier did not seem to know who "Bucky" was. One of his choppers came down and the Winter Soldier leaped to its landing gear and flew off, but not before dropping a small memento to Cap and his friends. The grenade rolled to their feet but they dove to safety, the explosion ringing out behind them. Luckily, all three survived the blast, with the Black Widow suffering only a few minor wounds.

VIDEO FOOTAGE OF CAPTAIN AMERICA'S FINAL CONFRONTATION WITH WINTER SOLDIER

PROPERTY OF
S.H.I.E.L.D.

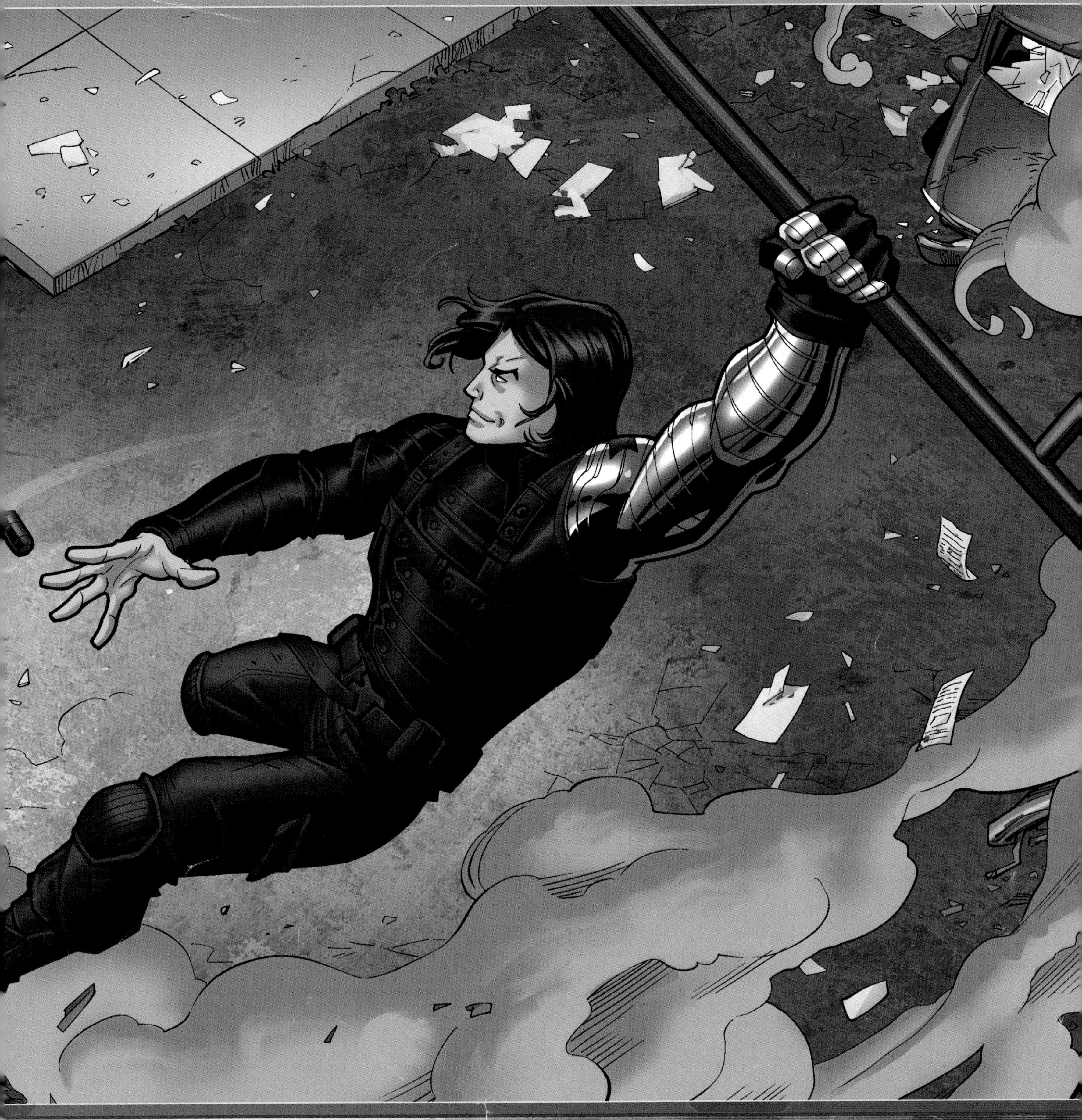

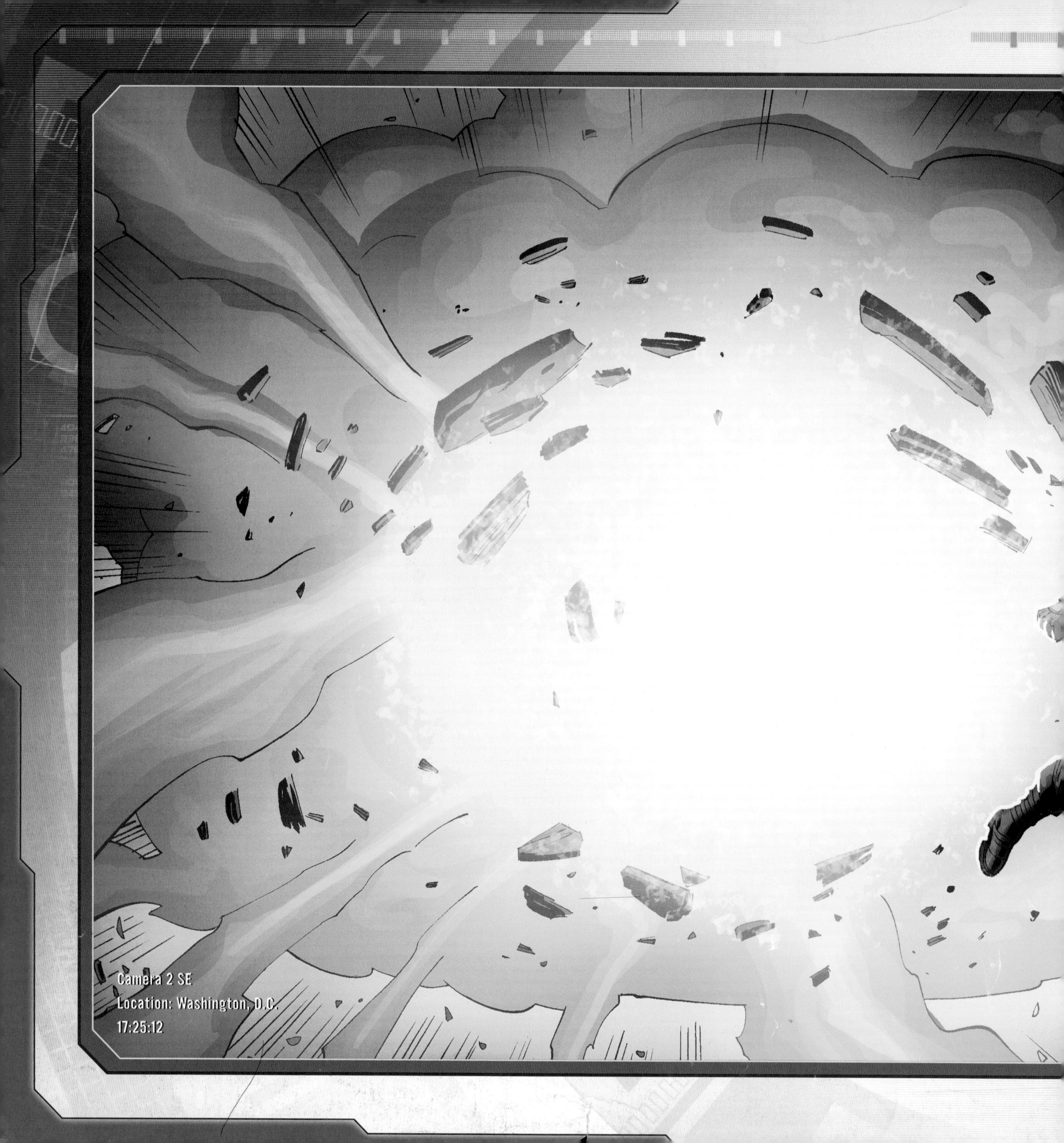
Camera 2 SE
Location: Washington, D.C.
17:25:12

Surveillance from a nearby CCTV captured this explosion during the battle with the Winter Soldier. Both **CAPTAIN AMERICA** and **BLACK WIDOW** survived, receiving minor cuts and bruises.

(798 DIDOT-PUNKTE=300MM)
DIDOT-PUNKT*8.3759398=MM
DIDOT-PUNKT*1.07001=PICA-PUNKT
DIDOT-PUNKT*8.0148057=INCH

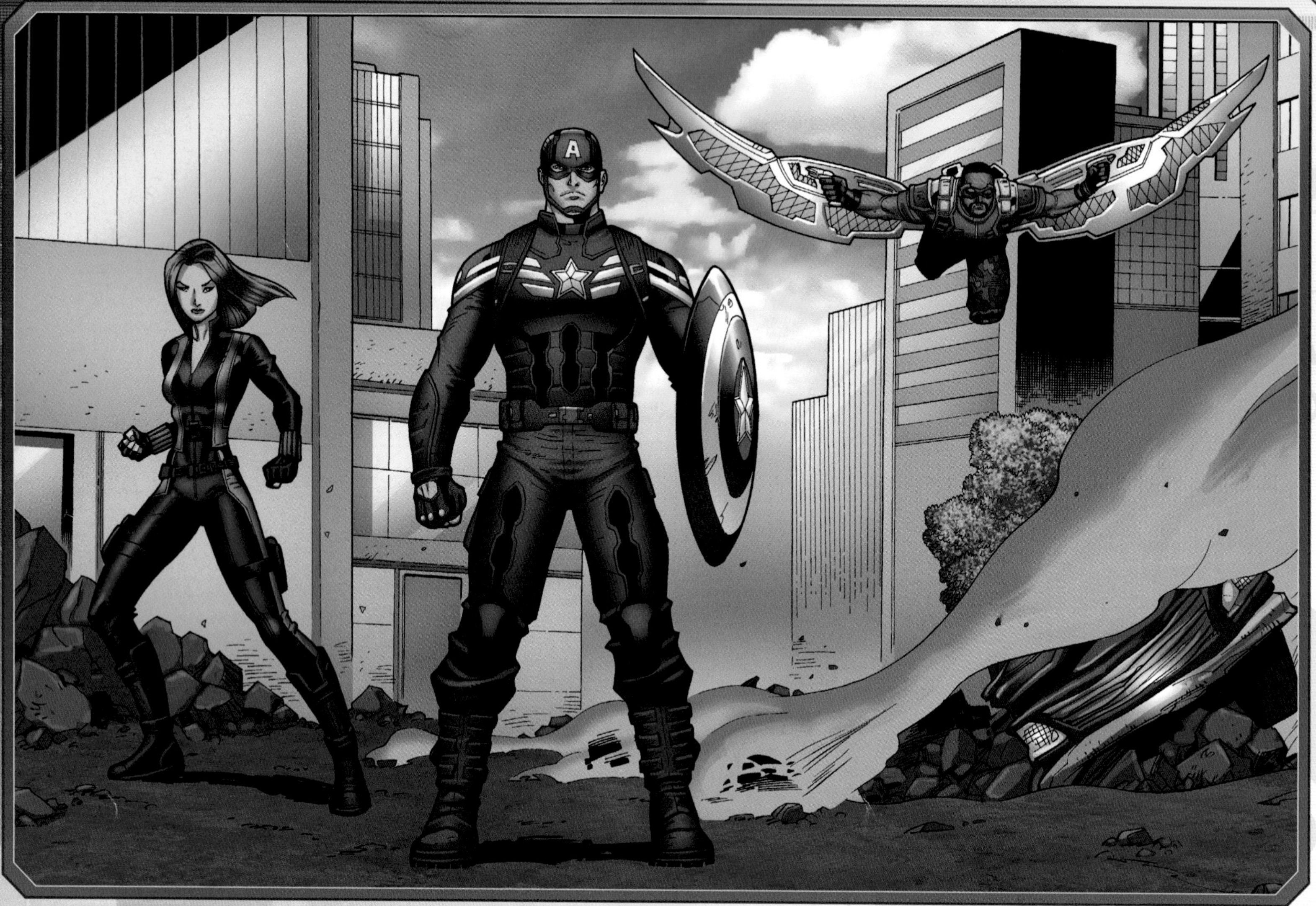

A NEW TEAM HAS FORMED: Captain America, the Black Widow, and the newest member, Falcon. Together they will work to stop the Winter Soldier and his team of mercenaries. We know Captain America will have questions. We also fear he may jeopardize our mission to stop the Winter Soldier due to his soft spot for his old friend. We have asked Agent Rumlow to follow Cap and make sure he follows protocol. We will closely monitor their mission as well as several other factors in this case. A meeting with the World Security Council is scheduled in the next few days. We think this report will suffice in informing them of the recent events. We thank you for your time in reviewing these files. Please report to ____________ when you are done and prepare for your next S.H.I.E.L.D. mission, which may involve finding the whereabouts of Nick Fury.